MAN
CANDY

Melanie Harlow

Copyright © 2016 by Melanie Harlow

All rights reserved. No part of this book may be reproduced in any form or by any electronic or mechanical means, including information storage and retrieval systems, without written permission from the author, except for the use of brief quotations in a book review.

Cover Design: Romantic Book Affairs
Cover Model: Dima Gornovskyi
Cover Photography: Kaspar Jack
Editing: Bethany Hagen, Nancy Smay
Publicity: Social Butterfly PR
Proofreading: Laura Foster Franks, Amanda Maria, Angie Owens
Formatting: Cait Greer

This is a work of fiction. References to real people, places, organizations, products and events are intended to provide a sense of authenticity and are used fictitiously. All characters, incidents, and dialogue are drawn the the author's imagination and not to be construed as real.

To Jenn, Kayti, Laurelin, and Sierra, for knowing the title of this book before I did and for understanding my need to touch the stove even after you've told me it's hot.

To the PQs…Crimson, Dena, Jaime, Laura, LeAnn, Margaret, Melanie, Melissa, and Rachel, for friendship, laughs, and delicious inspiration every day.

To my Harlots, who appreciate a nice piece of man candy.

And to Dima, for being so sweet.

On ne voit bien

qu'avec le coeur.

L'essentiel

est invisible

pour les yeux.

Antoine de Saint Exupery

CHAPTER ONE

Jaime

I was in the closet.

That's not a metaphor, by the way—I was literally, physically trapped in a closet. It wasn't even my closet; it was his. And it had that guy-closet smell, you know? Leather and cologne up front, base notes of sweat and testosterone lingering beneath. It wasn't entirely unpleasant. Actually, it was kind of hot in its uniquely masculine way, but I was in no mood and certainly no position to be turned on, crouching like a frog on top of some sneakers. My thighs were aching, I'd failed at pulling the hinged bi-fold doors all the way shut so I was totally visible through the crack, and I had the hiccups.

Did I mention I was drunk?

Oh, Jesus.

I'd set my wine glass down somewhere, hadn't I? What the hell had I been thinking? And why on earth had I gone for the fucking *closet* instead of the back door when he came in? I could have easily climbed the back steps to my balcony by now or even snuck around and come in the front door like I was just getting home from work or something. He didn't know I took the day off.

God, I was so *dumb*.

And it's not like I'd learned anything that interesting for all my sleuthing, except that there were two condoms missing from the twelve-count box of Trojans (size XL, if you're interested) in his nightstand drawer. I couldn't help but wonder if he'd used those since he'd moved in two weeks ago. I lived in the upper flat, so my bedroom was right above his, and I hadn't *heard* any sex noises coming through the floor, but then again, I worked all day long and sometimes well into the night…maybe he was the afternoon delight type.

He looked like that type. A meal you could enjoy morning, noon, or night. Like pigs in a blanket from The Pancake House.

Jealousy surged in me as I imagined him sticking his pig in some gorgeous blonde's blanket, whispering dirty things in her ear, making the bedsprings creak while the grown-ups of the world, the ones with real jobs, were hard at work. *Stop it. You have way bigger problems than who he fucks while you're at the office. Like how you're going to get out of here.*

Hiccup!

Oh, God. If he came into the bedroom, I was busted for sure.

Why was he home this early anyway? I happened to know he had a late class on Thursdays.

Had it been canceled because of the weather? Did he skip it because he didn't want to drive in the snow? What a pansy. We were only supposed to get, like, nine or ten inches. Practically nothing in Michigan! California must have softened him.

Hiccup!

Oh, fuck. Here he comes.

I heard him enter the room, and I tried to scoot back from the crack a little but fell onto his shoes and my foot bumped the door. *Shit!* Had he heard it? I held my breath as he walked past the closet and into the bathroom. A moment later I heard a belt being unbuckled. A zipper being lowered.

I rolled my eyes. *Jesus. Who doesn't shut the door when they pee? Men are such pigs.*

The toilet flushed, and I heard the faucet run. *At least he washes his hands.*

"So. How about a hot shower, gorgeous?"

His voice startled me, and I gasped, my heart whacking against my ribs. Was someone else here? Jesus, the only thing worse than being discovered by Quinn Rusek alone would be getting caught in his closet in front of some girl he'd brought home to fork in the shower. But I hadn't seen anyone else—was he talking to me?

Hiccup!

I clapped a hand over my mouth, frantically trying to think of an excuse for myself. My older brother Alex owned the house, and I was *sort of* the manager of the two apartments in it, so it wasn't *totally* unreasonable that I would be there. If only there were some kind of problem…

My brother asked me to check on the…um—

The heat. It's going to get really cold tonight.
The fridge. Is it still making that humming noise?
The plumbing. My sink is draining slowly.
Yeah, that was it. The plumbing thing.

And I heard someone come in, and I knew you had a late class so it scared me. I ran into the closet, completely freaked out!

Even better. Then he'd feel bad for scaring me. He was Alex's friend, though, so I could get caught in this lie if I wasn't careful. I'd have to call Alex right away. And I needed to get rid of these fucking hiccups.

"Yeah, I think getting hot, naked, and wet right now sounds like a good plan for a cold afternoon."

Smothering the squeal threatening to escape the back of my throat, I got on my hands and knees and poked my head out, *solely* for the purpose of ascertaining when it would be safe to make my escape, *not* because I was hoping to catch a glimpse of bare chest. Chiseled abs. XL dick.

Suddenly the navy blue Henley he'd been wearing flew out of the bathroom and landed on the floor in front of me. What the fuck? Was he getting undressed? He'd shut the bathroom door if he was going to get naked, right?

I leaned out farther.

"Fuck, this is gonna feel *goooooood.*"

And then it hit me—first his white T-shirt, square in the face, before landing atop the Henley—and second, the realization that he was messing with me.

I scrambled back into the closet.

That asshole knows I'm here. He's playing a game.

It was chicken—just like we used to play in my backyard pool, only with even less clothing. Well, if he thought I was going to give myself up just because he threatened to get naked, he could think again. I could do this all day.

I peeked out again.

Oh. My. God.

My mouth fell open. There he was—shirtless, jeans undone, *posing* in front of the mirror. Flexing his biceps. His pecs. His abs.

Every curve and line was perfection—the muscular thighs, the round ass, the narrow waist, the sculpted arms. Not that I was surprised. He'd quit modeling months ago, but he still worked out every day like it was his job. Then there were the gifts he was given—the things he didn't even have to work for. The brain-melting blue eyes, the unforgivable symmetry of his features, the angle of his jaw, the flawless skin.

After dropping a kiss onto each of his biceps—for fuck's sake, seriously?—he rubbed the back of his neck with one hand, then left it there while the other slid down his rippled abdomen and into the front of his underwear.

My breath caught.

Oh God, oh God, oh God. Would he really go that far?

I was sweating, my entire body on edge. At least my hiccups were gone.

But what should I do? Give myself up?

A good person would, said my conscience.

Was I a good person?

You're a drunk peeping Tom. All signs point to no.

So then I might as well see it through, right? After all, I'd made it this far. If I gave up now, he'd have something on me. *And* he'd have the upper hand. So maybe I'd call his bluff—see how far he'd actually go.

Great, now you're a perv as well as a snoop.

Maybe I was, because when he moved behind the half-open bathroom door and turned the water on, I crawled out a little bit farther to try for a better look. Could I catch his reflection in the mirror? Or see him through the crack?

Suddenly his jeans came sailing out, landing with a dull thump right in front of me.

And then his blue boxer briefs.

But I had no time to freak out, because the door opened wide and Quinn appeared, holding his hands over his crotch like a fucking fig leaf.

I gasped.

"So," he said, those blue eyes dancing. "Now what?"

Oh my fucking god.

The game of chicken…suddenly involved a cock.

CHAPTER TWO

Jaime

You might wonder how a perfectly sane, well-educated, completely logical woman such as myself ended up trapped in a man's closet.

I can explain.

When my brother Alex called and said he needed a favor, I thought he meant something for his upcoming nuptials, or as he liked to call it, "my big fat gay wedding." He's sort of like me in that he doesn't like a lot of fuss or fanfare, but his boyfriend Nolan had his heart set on a huge, splashy spring affair, so that's what they were having, come April fifth. (My brother is a much nicer person than I am.)

"What can I do for you?" My breath escaped my lips in silvery puffs as I crossed the frigid parking garage after work. It was about five o'clock, the earliest I'd left the office in two solid weeks, but it had been a long day and all I could think about was taking off my heels and pouring some wine. I still had work to do, but I could work from home. "Don't tell me—Nolan wants drone photography."

Alex laughed. "No."

"A pair of llamas?" I switched my cell to the other hand and unlocked my car. "A hot tub? Ariana Grande?"

"Why, can you get Ariana Grande?"

"If I can, does that mean I don't have to make a toast at the reception?"

"Nope."

"Then no, I can't." I slid behind the wheel and shut the door. "But if you'd like any celebrities of the automotive industry to make an appearance, I'm your girl."

Actually the marketing firm I worked for handled all kinds of clients, but since we were located in Detroit, many of them were businesses related to the auto industry.

"No, thanks. And anyway, it's not about the wedding. It's about the house."

"Oh?" I backed out of my spot and began the wide spiral down to the exit.

"Yeah. I might have a tenant, if you're OK with it."

"Of course I am. Sorry I haven't been more help with that. I know it stinks not to have rent coming in for downstairs. I was just so busy over the holidays, and then I had that huge presentation last week."

"That's OK. We're all busy, and eventually I *will* need your help, since this solution is really only temporary."

"Why's that?" I swiped my pass at the gate and eased onto the street, frowning as someone jaywalked right in front of me.

"Because he only needs a place to stay for a month while his condo is being finished. He wasn't supposed to move in until March first, but he leased his L.A. apartment starting first of the year. He's been living in a hotel downtown for two weeks, but he's sick of hotel living, hates the food and noise and how much it costs. Plus I think he's kind of lonely. I'd have him stay with us, but with the wedding and everything, it's really hectic at our house. And since the lower flat is already furnished, it seems like a perfect fit."

Lonely? "Wait, do you know this guy?"

"Yeah. It's..." He cleared his throat. Never a good sign. "It's Quinn."

I groaned.

"I know, I know, he's not your favorite, for whatever reason—"

"The *reason* is that he was a cocky, condescending asshole to me. Other than that, he's adorable."

"Come on, it's been ten years since the thing."

My eyelid twitched. Did he have to bring it up?

"Look, I'm sure he's forgotten all about it."

"*You* haven't. I can't even believe he told you."

"He felt like he had to. He knew you were upset and felt bad. He also wanted me to know he hadn't done anything to encourage it and never touched you. Mom and Dad were paying half his college tuition—what was he supposed to do?"

Kiss me back, dammit. Love me back.

Cringing, I recalled the way I had attempted to seduce my brother's closest friend at their joint graduation party at our house. The horrible details rushed into my mind as if a dam had burst...the wine I drank from a red Solo cup as I worked up the nerve to act on my crush. The artless way I shoved him into the downstairs bathroom and shut the door. The sound of my pounding heart as I pressed my bikini-clad body against him, lifting my lips toward his.

That awkward moment when I realized he wasn't into it.

Instead, he laughed.

That asshole *laughed* at me.

"Jaime, what the hell are you doing?" He turned on the light and stared at me, a look of bemused embarrassment on his face. His eyes were so beautiful—the kind of blue that made you shiver.

"Isn't it obvious?" Bravely, I put my hand on his crotch and felt his dick stir beneath the nylon of his damp swimsuit.

"Jesus. Stop it." More nervous laughter as he swatted my hand away.

"Why? You don't want this?" I blinked in confusion. Did he not feel the same pull I did when we were together? For months he'd been looking at me differently, teasing me more than usual, flirting with me in front of other people. Just an hour ago, he'd gotten handsy with me during a game of chicken in the pool—I was positive I'd felt his fingers graze my ass multiple times. Had I misread him?

He looked uncomfortable as he adjusted himself. "Look, you're like my little sister, and—"

"I'm only a year younger than you," I said, trying to sidle closer again. "And I'm definitely not your sister."

Backing away from me, he ran a hand through his dark blond hair, still a little wet from the pool. "Yeah, but...I'm sorry. I just can't."

And that's when I said it.

(Brace yourself.)

"But I love you."

He blinked. "What?"

"I'm in love with you, Quinn."

After a moment of stunned silence, during which neither of us blinked, he burst out laughing.

Shame and humiliation coursed through me. "Oh, God. Just forget it. Forget this ever happened." Without another word, I yanked the door open and ran from the bathroom straight to my bedroom, hot tears burning my eyes. How could I ever face him again?

Lucky for me, I never had to. I didn't know whether he'd avoided the house (me) on purpose, or whether he was just busy getting ready to leave for school, but a month after that, he left for UNC Chapel Hill without ever showing his face again.

But he hadn't even lasted a year there, because some model scout "discovered" him—every time I think of it, I roll my eyes—and plastered his stupid perfect face and hot body in catalogs and magazine ads and on shopping bags in stores that ripped off teenagers with overpriced clothes made in China. And he didn't even wear the clothes in all the pictures! Half the time he was nearly naked—it was ridiculous! (Didn't stop me from hoarding every one of those catalogs under my bed.)

Eventually, after I went to school and studied marketing, I realized that those pictures weren't necessarily meant to sell the clothes—they were selling an idea. A lifestyle. A *brand*.

That was also about the time I learned not to trust anything or anyone that looks too good to be true. Everyone is selling something—and if you're not selling, you're buying.

I'd bought enough assholery in my life already.

"Jaims, you there?" Alex sounded a little impatient.

"Yeah, I'm here," I said. "Sorry."

"So is it OK?"

I wanted to say no, and Alex had always told me I could have final say over who lived downstairs, but I couldn't. He barely charged me any rent and always came through with favors for me when I asked. "It's just one month?"

"One month," he promised. "And then he's out. Maybe even less, it just depends on when his new place is ready. You work so much anyway, I bet you'll barely even see each other."

"Good." I turned onto my street and noticed a black BMW with California plates parked at the curb. Lights on in the downstairs flat. "Jesus Christ, Alex…is he here already?"

"Ummm…I gotta go."

"What were you going to do if I said no?" I grumped, turning into the driveway. At least he hadn't blocked it. I'd probably have to clear out the other half of the garage and give him the second space, not that I had time to do that. *Already he's inconveniencing me.*

"Beg. Listen, I actually do have to run, we have an appointment with the florist that Nolan says I have to show up to, but do me a favor and be civil, OK? You heard about his mom."

Some of my irritation eased when I thought about his mom. She'd been our housekeeper for as long as I could remember, a single mother who'd also worked nights as a waitress, which left Quinn to fend for himself a lot. Growing up, he'd probably eaten more meals at our house than at his own, although I remember her being a fantastic cook. Our mother, with her graduate degree in biomedical engineering, could hardly boil water, but Mrs. Rusek used to bring over delicious homemade soups and bread and meatballs and pierogies, maybe because she felt guilty about how much time Quinn spent at our house.

"Yeah, Mom told me when it happened. Cancer, right? Like two years back?"

"Yeah. He brought her out to California for treatment, but I think he felt guilty that he'd worked and traveled so much she was able to hide her illness from him for so long. He told me she should have seen a doctor long before he took her. I think he blames himself."

"That's terrible." When I'd heard that Mrs. Rusek had died, I'd thought about reaching out to Quinn, even bought a sympathy card, but in the end I'd decided against it. The card was still at the bottom of a desk drawer at work.

"Then he was in Paris during those attacks. Kind of messed him up a little."

"I didn't know that."

"I didn't either, not until recently. We haven't spoken much over the last few years, we've both been so busy, but I think he really needs old friends right now."

"So he's moving back to Detroit for you?"

"No, but I think it's part of wanting to go back to when things were simpler or something. He said he's been feeling kind of lost and wants to ground himself again. Make sure he's doing the right things with his life."

"Hmm." Inside the garage, I turned off the car, disquieted by the way my heart was thumping. It had been ten years since I'd seen him—and probably at *least* a month since I'd stalked his Instagram—how annoying that the thought of being next to him again was doing things to me. "So did he quit modeling altogether?"

"That's the impression I got."

"Maybe he's lost his looks," I said hopefully. "Or gained fifty pounds."

Alex laughed. "I doubt it. And I really have to go, Jaims. But why don't you go in and say hello? I'm sure he'd love to catch up."

I sniffed. "No, thanks. I'll keep my distance." My dignity had suffered enough at his hands.

"Have it your way, sweet pea," he said, using our dad's nickname for me. "Thanks for this."

We hung up, and I took a minute to gather myself before going into the house. There was a chance I could get in without seeing him, although we'd share a front and side entrance. Both doors led to a hallway; at the side door were steps leading to the basement, and at the front door were the stairs to my flat and a door to his living room.

I walked around to the front, my legs trembling. Maybe he wouldn't hear me come in, and I could get up to my apartment without talking to him. *Stop being ridiculous. It's been ten years.* Maybe Alex was right and he wouldn't even remember that night. Maybe he wouldn't even want to talk to me. Maybe we'd just ignore each other for a month.

No chance.

Before I even got the key in the lock, the door was pulled open and there he was, all huge grin and open arms. "Sweet pea!" he exclaimed, like we were long-lost pals reunited at last.

Any hopes I'd harbored about his good looks being the result of countless hours of retouching were immediately dashed. He was even more gorgeous and vibrant in person than in print, a fact I found grossly unfair. I frowned as he scooped me up in his arms and practically dragged me over the threshold into the hall. My God, his body was so *hard*. Hugging me was probably like squeezing a marshmallow. I wasn't exactly overweight, but I was short enough that every extra ounce showed. Muscle tone was pretty much nonexistent.

"It's so good to see you, Jaime," he said. "You look great."

"You too," I said before I could stop myself. I didn't want him to think I still cared—in fact, I wanted him to know I wasn't fooled by his charm. I wasn't that silly little girl anymore, the one who'd doodled his name in her notebooks and blushed when he said hi at school and cried herself to sleep when he asked another girl to his prom. That silly little girl was gone, and in her place was a confident, smart, professional woman who knew her worth and, even better, the truth about love. No more stars in her eyes.

But why did he have to be so hot?

OK, pull yourself together. No drooling.

"I'm so glad this worked out." Quinn let me go but stood too close, his feet planted wide and his arms crossed over his chest. He wore jeans, a gray knit pullover that hugged his muscular chest and arms, and his feet were bare. His hair was damp and messy on top, just like it had been the last time I'd seen him in person. His full lower lip made me want to bite it. Maybe even draw blood.

"Sorry, I just got out of the shower," he said sheepishly, ruffling his hair. "Want to come in and catch up? Or maybe go out for a drink? I just need to throw some shoes on."

"No." Trying desperately to shove the image of him in the shower from my mind, I elbowed past him and trudged up the stairs. My cheeks were hot, which meant they were probably turning scarlet. They ruined my poker face every time.

"Come on, it's Friday!"

"I have work to do." *He was naked a few minutes ago. And wet.*

"Did you have a bad day?"

"No." *Rivulets of water streaming over those muscles.*

"You already have plans tonight?"

"No." *Steam rising as he stroked himself beneath the spray.*

"You don't love me anymore?"

I froze as the shower fantasy exploded into bits, replaced by a humiliation that paralyzed me, one foot on the top step, one hand on the banister. Slowly, I turned my head and glared at him over one shoulder.

Now the grin cocked up on one side. "Because you used to, you know. You told me."

"You need to forget about that."

"Have you?"

"Yes," I snapped. "That was a long time ago. Back when I was young and impressionable and believed in love."

His brows went up. "You don't believe in love anymore?"

"Not the romantic kind. That's a fantasy used to sell things like lipstick and roses and diamonds."

"Pretty jaded for twenty-seven, aren't you?"

I resumed heading up the stairs. "I'm not jaded, Quinn. I'm just a realist." *And I've been burned before, trusting guys way less attractive than you.*

He said nothing more, and I let myself into my flat. As soon as the door was shut behind me, I leaned back against it, exhaling and fanning my face.

He still got to me. That was *so aggravating*.

I mean, how was I supposed to sleep at night? Quinn Rusek was one fine piece of man candy, and I had a sweet tooth for him that wouldn't quit.

But he'd made fun of me! Again! A nice guy would have at least pretended not to remember what

I'd said. Or maybe apologized for humiliating me. Or not have brought it up at all!

What an asshole.

A hot asshole—the worst kind.

Curse you, Alex, and your generous heart.

And curse you, Quinn, for getting under my skin again. You stay away from me.

But a traitorous little part of me hoped he wouldn't.

(Bet you can guess which part.)

CHAPTER
THREE

Quinn

Damn, she was gorgeous.

Standing there at the bottom of the steps, I couldn't stop smiling. I heard the door to her flat slam shut and then a thump, as if she'd collapsed against it. Poor thing. I probably shouldn't have brought up the night she told me she loved me, but she was acting so cool, brushing me off like that. If it wasn't for those flaming red cheeks, I might have thought her disinterest was genuine and just let it go.

But I hadn't been able to resist trying to get a rise out of her—to see if that girl I knew was still there underneath that frosty exterior, the little spitfire with the big eyes and bigger mouth, the one who believed me when I told her hanging by her knees from a tree branch would stretch her bones and make her legs longer, the one who'd gotten so mad when she found out I'd made it up that she'd stomped on my foot, told me she hated my guts, and vowed she'd never talk to me again. (She lasted two days.)

Recalling the way she'd stomped up the stairs just now, I laughed a little. *Oh yeah, she's still there.*

And what about that girl who'd followed me into the bathroom and put her hands on me…was she still there? The one who had no idea how tempting she was, how badly I'd wanted to kiss her, how uncomfortable I'd been with the feelings I had for her. I'd practically lived at the Owens house growing up—Alex was my closest friend, and Jaime was his younger sister! A good friend just didn't do that. And Mr. and Mrs. Owens had been so generous to my mother and me. For fuck's sake, they were paying more than half my college tuition. Even at eighteen, I was old enough to recognize there was a line there that should not be crossed.

But God, I'd wanted to. I'd wanted to cross that line with every part of my body, hard and often. I'd thought about it for months, been tempted a million times. In fact, I'd almost asked Alex if he'd be OK with my asking her to the prom, but chickened out. Instead I'd asked Danica Newman, and while she blew me at the hotel party afterward, I imagined she was Jaime and came so fast I almost forgot to give a warning. But that was as close as I'd ever thought I'd get to the real thing.

So of course when she came on to me in the bathroom during the party, I'd reacted badly. I hadn't meant to laugh, but what else was there to do? I was off guard and nervous and so fucking turned on, I couldn't help it. It was so unfair, like God was testing me, seeing if I was really worthy of her family's generosity. The *one* girl I couldn't have was the one I wanted, and there she was with her hand on my dick, her perfect tits filling out that red bikini, and that pouty little mouth begging to be kissed (seriously, the number of times I've jerked off to the memory of her in that red bikini is staggering). I'd been so close to giving in.

And then she told me she loved me, and I lost it.

It was just so sweet, and her eyes were so sincere. She *trusted* me. She'd have done anything I wanted her to.

I couldn't take advantage of it.

Believe me, in my fantasies, that night went down a whole different way, but I stand by my choice to be a gentleman.

Except now I was being punished for it!

OK, maybe I shouldn't have poked at her just now, but fuck, that's what felt natural with us—I hadn't seen her in a while, but sometimes being with someone from your past is like going home again. No matter how long it's been, you don't forget the way.

I went back into my temporary digs and sat on the couch, thinking about the last ten years, and how far from home they'd taken me. Although modeling had never been my dream job, I'd jumped at the opportunity to make the kind of money the scout had promised—and he hadn't lied.

The amount of money I made shocked me—enough to live well in L.A. and pay off all my mother's debt, make it so she'd never have to clean houses again (although I couldn't convince her to leave her house or her restaurant job). Enough to cover all her medical expenses after I discovered how sick she was. Enough to make the end of her life as peaceful and full as possible.

But not enough to buy her time.

It made me pause and take stock. Ask myself some questions.

Life was short—what did I want to do with mine? What did I want to learn, accomplish, leave behind? What memories would I cherish when it was time to look back? What would matter most?

The amount of money in my bank account?

The number of beautiful women I'd fucked?

The square footage of my house?

As impressive as those figures were, I realized they'd be meaningless in the end. And after the bombings in Paris, where I witnessed firsthand how quickly and cruelly life can be snuffed out, I knew I had to change things. I just didn't know how.

Alex had been my first call.

We hadn't been as close in the last ten years of our lives as we'd been in the first eighteen, but we had the kind of friendship that didn't require a quota of check-ins or a constant stream of updates. He might have grown up in a six-bedroom Tudor with a three-car garage and a pool in the yard while I grew up in a tiny two-bedroom bungalow on a street lined with the century-old homes of servants from another era, but we *got* each other.

He'd always be there for me; I'd always be there for him. Period. I'd already been planning on coming in for his wedding, but he'd been the one to suggest maybe moving back for a time, or trying school again, and as soon as he said it, I knew it was the right idea.

The last two months had been a whirlwind of buying the condo, leasing my L.A. home, shipping my stuff to Detroit for storage, cancelling what jobs I could get out of, moving into a hotel downtown, and enrolling in a couple classes at Wayne State. I'd hardly had time to breathe.

But things were starting to settle a little, and living here would be so much nicer than staying in a cold, impersonal hotel room for the next few weeks while I waited for the work on my condo to be completed. I'd jumped at the chance when Alex offered last week—especially when he told me Jaime lived upstairs. I'd been really excited to see her again.

Clearly, the feeling was not mutual.

I frowned. Should I apologize?

While I thought it over, I returned to what I'd been doing when I saw her pull in, which was unpacking the few books, pictures, and mementos I'd kept out of storage. A framed photo of my mom when she was younger, and one of us together on the beach in La Jolla before she died. Most of the books were texts for this semester; I was taking a history course, a political science seminar, and a math class.

But I also had my senior year yearbook, which I'd found while going through boxes in my mom's attic last week. She'd given the little house to her church in her will, and they used it to provide housing to women and children who needed a safe place to stay, which my mother would have loved. I'd quickly had all her personal things boxed and stored in the attic, and I'd paid for the necessary renovations, but I hadn't been back there since she left and figured it was time to clean out the place once and for all.

I'd had no idea how much crap was up there.

I swear to God, you'd have thought my mother grew up during the Depression or something. The woman saved *everything*. It was going to take me months to get through it all, and even though most of it would be junk to anyone else, I didn't want to just throw stuff out without looking at it. It hadn't been junk to her.

Picking up the yearbook, I sat on the couch and opened it to the front cover. It was covered with writing, and I wondered if Jaime had signed it somewhere. I didn't see her name anywhere in the front, so I turned to the back, which was also full of signatures, farewells, and phone numbers, but not hers. Disappointed, I flipped to the page displaying her junior year photo and saw that she'd written to me there—neat cursive lettering along the white borders of the page.

Quinn, you will probably never see this because you think yearbooks are stupid and you didn't ask me to sign it anyway. (I took it in study hall when you weren't looking. You are over in the corner flirting with someone, surprise surprise.) Well, I just wanted to say I hope you have a great summer and even though I am still mad at you for what you said about how to grow taller (I still can't believe I fell for that), I'm glad we are friends and I will really miss you next year. Maybe I can come visit you!!! I think we could have a good time... Love, J

I closed the book, feeling that intense attraction for her resurface. Leaning back on the couch, I stared up at the ceiling. It was quiet up there. Would I be able to hear her television? Her phone calls? Her shower running? What was she doing now? Changing out of her work clothes? I thought about her sliding out of that pencil skirt she'd been wearing, and blood rushed between my legs. I loved a pencil skirt and heels on a woman. Feminine and sexy, but strong too. Was that what grown-up Jaime was like?

Before I could think it through, I got off the couch and went up the stairs, knocking three times. Sure, she'd brushed me off earlier, but I loved a challenge, and I wanted to get to know her. Maybe I could charm my way into her good graces.

Truth be told, I'm pretty good at charming my way into tight spaces.

CHAPTER
FOUR

Quinn

She opened the door wearing a gray Detroit Tigers T-shirt with the neck cut out, light blue flannel pajama pants, and fluffy pink socks. Without her heels, she was even shorter than I remembered, and I had to fight the urge to tease her again. But fuck, she was pretty, even with that scowl. Heart-shaped face, big green eyes, puffy pink lips. I'd forgotten about that dimple in her chin—fucking adorable.

"What."

"I came for a visit, like you said in my yearbook."

She cocked her head. "Huh?"

"In my yearbook. You wrote that you wanted to visit me at school. You said, 'I think we could have a good time.' I agree. Let's do it." Dropping my chin, I gave her my most winning smile.

Irresistible, right?

She shrank back, wrinkling her nose. "What the hell is that? Your Flynn Ryder smolder?"

"Who's Flynn Ryder?"

She rolled her eyes. "He's from Tangled, the Rapunzel movie?"

"Sorry. I missed it. So does he get in her pants?"

"Not before she hits him over the head with a frying pan."

"Ouch." I leaned right and left, checking her hands. "Since I don't see any cookware in your grasp, is it safe to come in?"

She eyeballed me and crossed her arms. "Why do you want to come in?"

"I don't know, actually." I mirrored her posture, crossing my arms. "It's not like the welcome has been all that warm."

Her arms fell, and her scowl abated slightly. But just slightly. "Sorry. I'm just…sort of a private person. And it's been a long day."

"No problem." Flashing my palms at her, I turned for the steps. "Just thought I'd try again to be friendly. It really is good to see you. Sorry to bother you." I hotfooted it down the stairs, figuring I'd play a little harder to get from here on out. Maybe she liked a challenge too.

"Quinn, wait."

Bingo.

Halfway down, I looked up to see her hovering on the landing, hugging her stomach, her juicy bottom lip caught between her teeth. Was it wrong that I noticed her nipples were hard and poked through her thin cotton shirt? *Don't stare at her tits, asshole. You want her to invite you in, you have to at least appear gentlemanly.*

"Don't go," she said. "I guess we could…hang out a little."

I waited for her to go on, to invite me in, but she just stood there.

"OK. Should we hang out on the steps? Or would you like to come down? Boxes are everywhere, but—"

"No, no." She sighed, and her eyes closed briefly. "You can come up."

Grinning victoriously, I went back up the stairs and followed her in, shutting the door behind me. The upper flat appeared to be laid out just like the lower, with the living room at the front, dining room and kitchen in the middle, and two bedrooms and bathrooms at the back. It had the same neutral carpeting and paint colors, although her furniture was nicer, and she'd added feminine things like pillows and flowers and candles. It smelled nice too, sort of sweet and flowery. Or was that her?

"I was just about to open some wine. Do you want some?" She put her hair in a ponytail as she shuffled into the kitchen. It was dark and wavy and fell past her shoulders, long enough to wrap around my fist if I—

Oh, shit. She just asked me a question, didn't she?

"Sure." I leaned against the doorframe and watched her wrestle with the corkscrew and bottle, admiring her from behind. Her sloppy clothing hid her curves, but her shirt rode up and her pants slipped down just enough for me to see a ribbon of pale skin between them. My dick, which had already noticed she wasn't wearing a bra beneath her shirt, showed even more interest in finding out if she had underwear on. Clearly it remembered the lost opportunity from years ago and wanted to punish me.

"Like red?" She had to rise up on tiptoe to reach the wine glasses, and I adjusted myself while she wasn't looking.

"Of course. Antioxidants, resveratrol...what's not to like?"

"Oh, you're one of *those*." Shaking her head, she poured the wine. "Figures."

"One of those what?"

"One of those people who drink one glass of red wine a night because it's healthy, not because it tastes good and makes you feel like you can get through another day without hitting someone with a frying pan." She gave me a pointed look over her shoulder.

I laughed. "Can't a person do both? Enjoy something because it tastes good and it's good for them?"

"I guess. But there are very few things that fit that description, at least for me. Everything I like is bad. Here." Handing me a glass, she brought hers to her lips. "Ahh," she said after a good long drink. "That's better."

"What do you like that's bad for you?"

"Bacon. Butter. Chocolate. Wine. Ice cream. Bread. Chips. Cocktails. Things that are battered and fried." She took another drink. "Should I go on?"

"That's your diet?" I set my wine glass on the counter and opened her fridge. "My God, how do you live?" I asked her, shaking my head. "Ketchup, mustard, jelly, eggs, butter, and pickles…what is that, olives?"

"Yeah, but those are for my martinis."

"At least you have milk."

"It's probably expired. But I do like cereal for dinner sometimes. And sometimes I put it in my coffee, if I don't have cream."

"Jesus. No meat, no vegetables…" I opened the crisper. "One lonely apple."

"I've been busy," she said, her tone defensive. "And no one asked you to look in my fridge, anyway. Get out of there." She kicked the crisper shut, closed the fridge and leaned back against it, an adorably defiant look on her face.

I shook my head. "No wonder your growth is stunted. You know, I was lying about the tree thing, but I do think if you ate healthier, you'd feel better. Maybe even grow a little."

"This is why I didn't want to let you in."

"OK, OK. Suit yourself." I should have stopped there, but something in me loved the way I could still rile her up. "But I'd be happy to share some of my tips for healthy eating and living with you if you'd like. Do you exercise?" I took her face in my hands, tilted it this way and that. Her complexion was beautiful, her skin like porcelain. "And look how pale you are—are you inside all day?"

"It's January in Michigan!" she said, leaning away from me. "Of course I'm pale!"

"Well, a brisk walk outside won't kill you. Vitamin D is important." I grabbed my wine off the counter and took a sip to cover the grin on my face.

She glared at me. "This conversation is over. And if you don't stop making fun of me, this visit is over too."

"I didn't mean any offense by that, Jaime. You look perfect. You're beautiful."

"That's not what you said a minute ago."

"What I said wasn't based on how you look—it was based on what you eat. Mostly."

She cocked her head. "Why do you care what I eat, anyway? You haven't spoken to me in ten years."

"I know. But you're like a little sister to me, and I—"

She groaned and flashed one palm at me. "Please. Not that again."

"Sorry." I had to smile at the blush painting her face. "How about friends? Can we be friends?"

"I don't know." She eyed me with skepticism, swirling her wine.

"Oh, you're one of *those*," I teased.

"One of those what?"

"One of those people who believe men and women can't be friends." Leaning back against the counter opposite the fridge, I took another drink. "At least, not if they're attracted to one another."

"I never said I was attracted to you!" she blustered. "I'm sure you've had women all over the world fall at your feet, but I'm not one of them. At least—" She fidgeted, then stood a little taller. Well, taller for *her*. "Not now. Not anymore."

"Of course not."

"Are you laughing at me?" she asked indignantly.

"I would never. I'm just happy to see you again. I want to get to know you." (I was totally laughing at her.)

"And I never said men and women couldn't be friends, either." She jerked her chin at me.

Fuck, that dimple. I wanted to kiss it. Actually, I wanted to rub it with the tip of my cock, but I tried not to think about that too hard. What was she saying now?

"I have lots of male friends," she insisted.

"Oh. My mistake." While I calmly took another sip of wine (this took some effort, since I couldn't stop thinking about my dick on her chin), she gulped hers, clearly flustered. "So tell me about grown-up Jaime. What does she do?"

"I'm a social media specialist at a marketing firm."

"Do you like it?"

"For the most part. Sometimes I wish I got to do more of the creative stuff, more of the research and whole campaign strategy, but I've only been at this a couple years. I get that I have to work my way up."

"What do you do for fun? Hang out with all your male friends?"

She rolled her eyes. "My closest friends are actually women. Do you remember Claire French and Margot Lewiston from school?"

I nodded. "Yes. You three together were nothing but trouble back then."

"Ha. We're less trouble now, but still together."

"That's awesome, to have friends like that, to be so close for so many years."

She tilted her head. "Didn't you have good friends in L.A.?"

I shrugged. "I had a few. But I traveled a lot."

"What about a girlfriend?"

"One or two. Nothing serious."

She sighed dramatically. "I suppose it's hard to have a serious girlfriend what with young women throwing themselves at you all the time."

I nodded. "And older women too. Don't forget them."

"Come on, older women like your bathroom mirror selfies? What's with that, anyway? You're so vain you have to capture yourself in a towel capturing yourself in a towel?"

I cocked a brow. "Now who's making fun? And does this mean you follow me on Instagram?"

She lifted her shoulders, like she couldn't remember if she did or not, but her cheeks looked like two splotches of wine on a white linen tablecloth. "I follow a lot of people."

"Right." God, she was fucking delightful. So different from most women I met—so determined to put me in my place. "And what about you? Boyfriend?"

She snorted, lifting her glass. "No. I don't do relationships."

"And why's that?"

"I work a ton, I don't like anything to interfere with my girl time or my alone time, and I'm not a good girlfriend. Every guy I date more than a few times wants more than I can give."

"More what? More time? More emotion? More sex?"

"Let's go with time and emotion," she said, looking me in the eye. "I'm all for no-strings sex. But like I told you earlier, I don't believe in love."

"Oh, that's right. You did tell me that. And is this something you announce on the first date?"

"*No*, smartass, it isn't. But I don't think it hurts anyone to be honest up front about where dating me can and cannot go. So I lay it all out there."

I nodded, setting my wine glass aside. "OK, then. Lay it on me."

"Why?"

"Maybe I want to take you on a date."

She made a face. "I'm not going on a date with *you*."

"Why not? My mom said I'm a good catch."

"I don't trust you."

"That doesn't seem fair."

"I don't want a boyfriend."

"I said one date."

Her head tilted and she gave me a sassy look. "Maybe I'm not attracted to you."

Liar. There's something here and you know it. I gave her a slow smile. "Maybe."

"So I'm sure you're not used to hearing this, but you keep your hands to yourself. Got it?"

It was a bluff, and I couldn't resist calling it.

I moved slowly, closing the space between us in three steps and caging her against the fridge with a hand on either side of her face. My upper body barely brushed against hers. I stared her down hard, felt the quick rise and fall of her chest. "Got it, sweet pea."

She hesitated, but then lifted her chin slightly, daring me to kiss her. We stood like that a few more seconds, each of us waiting for the other to back down or give in.

A game of chicken—just like the old days.

But despite her tempting mouth, I quickly strategized that kissing her now would be a mistake. The little minx had just told me she wasn't attracted to me—I couldn't give her what she wanted yet. I hadn't missed what she said about no-strings sex (and believe me, my dick had taken that as an invitation and went looking for his party hat), but I didn't want that from her.

I backed off. "Well, thanks for the drink. This was nice."

She blinked, her icy facade in a puddle at her feet. "You're leaving?"

"Yeah, I should get back downstairs and finish unpacking."

"Oh. OK." She cleared her throat. "Yeah, that's good. I actually have some work to do tonight."

I walked out of the kitchen, glad she was behind me and couldn't see the grin on my face. In the living room, she shouldered past me and pulled open the door. Then she stood behind it like it was some sort of shield, making it impossible to even hug her.

"Thanks for the wine. Don't drink too much, now." I gave her ponytail a tug before heading out the door, like I used to when she was just Alex's little sister, gratified at the annoyed expression it put on her face.

"You're welcome," she snapped, letting me know I was anything but.

The sound of her door slamming behind me made me smile even bigger.

She was something else. Feisty as she was back then and ten times hotter.

I bet she's a firecracker in bed. I bet she likes to be on top and call the shots, which I'd happily allow her to do, but that also means it would be an even bigger challenge—and maybe even more fun—to subdue her.

For a moment my mind wandered to a place where I had her restrained, blindfolded, and on her knees.

Jesus.

I had to stop halfway down the stairs and adjust my pants again.

Back in my apartment, I finished unpacking and tried to study, but it was useless—I couldn't stop thinking about her. And not just sexual stuff, either.

OK yeah, mostly sexual stuff.

But I didn't want to just fuck her. She wasn't some random girl at a bar in Prague I'd never see again (although we had fun that night, didn't we, Veronika?). She was someone from my past I felt a connection with. Someone I wanted to know better now. Someone who mattered to me.

Eventually my stomach started growling, so I went to the store for a few groceries, and when I got home, I noticed her living room lights were still on. I thought about knocking on her door, inviting her down for chicken Caesar salad. ("You *have* heard of salad before, right? It's, like, lettuce and a few other delicious, healthy things in a bowl?")

But I didn't do it, because I knew she'd have turned me down. I was pretty good at reading people, and I had the feeling Jaime was a woman who liked things on her own terms, and if you weren't willing to meet her terms, you could fuck right off—especially if your name was Quinn Rusek.

It made me smile.

I mean, she'd clearly wanted me to kiss her in the kitchen, if only to prove that I was the kind of guy who couldn't keep my hands to myself.

But the more I thought about it, the more I was glad I'd backed away. I could play the long game with her, especially if the game was chicken.

When I kissed her—and I was going to kiss her—it was going to be on *my* terms.

I wanted her to come to me and admit she felt that spark. I wanted her to give me another chance. I wanted to do things differently with her.

But first, I wanted to make her sweat a little.

Then I wanted to make her sweat a lot.

CHAPTER FIVE

Jaime

I was fuming.

The nerve.

The fucking *nerve* of the guy.

He'd wanted to kiss me, I knew he had—so why didn't he do it? Or had I misread him again? God, why was Quinn Rusek so hard for me to figure out? For crying out loud, I had degrees in psychology and marketing! I made a living out of studying people and strategizing how to make them behave a certain way. I was *good* at it. How did he have me so off my game?

Now I was even more embarrassed than I'd been in the first place. Jesus, this was twice now he'd turned me down. *Twice!*

I flopped facedown on my couch.

I'd been so proud of myself for playing it nice and cool, then I ruined everything by trying to get him to kiss me!

Ugh, he was probably downstairs laughing his ass off, and up here I was all hot and bothered by how close he'd been to me. Even closer than the night of the doomed seduction, his entire body grazing against mine.

Holy smoke, his body.

I was dying to know if it would look as good naked as it appeared in photos. Did it really have all those ridges and lines? Was his skin really that smooth and perfect? He'd been so close I could smell his soap.

Or maybe that was his hair product. Yeah, he looked like the kind of guy to have hair products—pomades and waxes and gels and pastes—I bet he spent more time in front of the mirror than I did.

Whatever it was, he'd smelled good enough to eat. I'd wanted to take a big old bite out of him. And I would have too—that's what made me even madder. If he'd have kissed me, I'd have dropped that wine glass and jumped up on him like bacon grease hopping off the pan. We'd probably be fucking each other's brains out on the kitchen floor by now, which sounded like a pretty good time.

So why hadn't he done it? Was it his mission in life to torture me? Make me hot for him only to reject me again? OK fine, so ten years ago he'd been worried about crossing the line because of Alex or my parents or whoever, but what was his problem tonight?

He doesn't have a problem. You do.

I howled into the cushion, kicking my feet and pounding my fists like a toddler throwing a tantrum. I didn't care what Alex said—Quinn Rusek was a sadist. And this was the last time—*the last time*—I was going to let him make a fool out of me. No way would I agree to a date with him.

He'd probably stand me up anyway!

I dragged myself into the kitchen and poured another glass of wine (well, it was probably more like two glasses, but since it fit in a single big glass, I'll call it one), then took my laptop into the guest room where I had my home office set up. I opened it, but instead of going to client files, I went right to Quinn's Instagram account. His last post was a selfie (of course, did he take any other kind of picture?) with the MacArthur Bridge behind him that looked as if it had been taken on Belle Isle. Snow blanketed the ground and chunks of ice floated in the river, which stood out in the picture because it was the exact blue of his eyes. He wore a navy baseball cap with a white Old English D on the front, and the caption was just a hashtag: #BeautifulDetroit.

To the right were all the usual comments from friends, followers, and creepers, everything from a gazillion smiley-faces with hearts for eyes or blowing heart-kisses to marriage proposals, actual compliments like **wow gorgeous pic**, and just plain weird crap like **do you like helicopter rides?** next to a banana emoji. Lots of the comments were not in English, and I wondered if Quinn had actually picked up any foreign languages during the last ten years with all his traveling for work. I wondered what countries he'd been to, which were his favorites and why, and where he'd like to visit again.

But I couldn't ask him those questions. Or any questions at all. My only mission for the next month where Quinn Rusek was concerned was to avoid him. Protect my dignity. And if my curiosity (or my desire) threatened to get the better of me, as it often did, I'd remind myself how I'd felt the night of the graduation party—rejected, ashamed, foolish. Since then, I'd been lied to, cheated on, and taken advantage of, but I'd never felt as heartbroken as I had the night Quinn turned me down. Why should I invite him to hurt me again?

Because he would. I knew he would.

They always do.

Don't be drunk and depressing. Get to work.

After a big gulp of wine to fortify my strength, I closed out of Instagram without even scrolling down (I deserved a medal) and opened my work files, looking over my notes from a meeting I'd had with a new client this afternoon. My task was to create some content ideas that would increase brand awareness and grow potential customer engagement—pretty standard stuff.

But it was impossible to concentrate knowing he was right beneath me. Every noise had me wondering.

What was that thump? Did he drop something?

I hear hangers on the closet rod in the guest room down there. I bet he has so many clothes he needs two closets. Total peacock. (Never mind that I used two full closets too.)

Rod. Now I wonder what his rod is like.

Was that the front door closing? Where's he going?

He's back. Wonder if he got dinner. I'm hungry.

The toilet just flushed. Great, now I'm thinking about his rod again.

His bedroom TV is on. Wonder what he likes to watch at night. What if it's porn? (That thought intrigued me so much, I went into my bedroom, lay down on the floor and pressed my ear to the hardwood.)

Nope. He's catching up on Game of Thrones. Bummer. But also cool, because GoT is awesome. Wonder who his favorite character is. For a moment, I entertained a little fantasy about the two of us watching together, maybe even sitting on the couch, with a pizza and a bottle of wine on the table.

No. I bet he doesn't even eat pizza.

Mmm, pizza.

I love pizza.

Hauling my tipsy ass off the ground, I gave up on work and went into the kitchen, where I found a French bread pizza in the freezer. I debated using the oven, since frozen pizza nuked in the microwave always turns out a bit soggy and flaccid, but decided I was too hungry to be picky. While it cooked, I studied the box. "French bread" was a bit of a stretch, and I wondered if it had been a marketing idea. ("I know!" I imagined someone saying in an advertising meeting. "Let's call it French, that sounds fancier. Maybe they can make the one edge a bit bullet-shaped so it vaguely resembles a baguette, but make it wider, like a baguette after a piano was dropped on it.")

When the microwave dinged, I took my dinner back to my desk—along with another glass of wine…OK, the rest of the bottle—and while I ate, I researched the history of French bread pizza. According to the Internet, where all Great Truths are discovered, Stouffer's bought (or maybe copied) the idea from a guy who ran a food truck at Cornell University, starting in 1960. I filed that interesting yet useless maybe-fact away in my brain, which housed an entire library of those things, and tried focusing on my client again.

Needless to say, after that much wine, I ended up back on Instagram, and was rabidly scrolling through Quinn's account (Jesus, did the guy *ever* take a bad pic? And did he get to keep all the little underpants he wore in these photo shoots or did he have to give them back? Like, if I snooped in his underwear drawer, would it be full of colorful banana hammocks or just plain old boxer briefs?) when my phone vibrated. I glanced down and saw a text from Claire, one of my two closest friends.

I need one of you to put ORC into motion.

Got it, I typed back.

Let me know if you need me, Margot responded.

ORC stood for Operation Rescue Claire. It meant I had to call her in five minutes with some reason she needed to leave the terrible date she was on, immediately. We'd set it up two years ago among our friends after it became clear that NO is not in Claire's vocabulary, so she says yes to all dates. She doesn't like to hurt people's feelings, and besides that, she genuinely believes that her soul mate is out there, poor thing. She's the kind of girl who thinks love at first sight is possible, people always mean what they say, and Jack somehow survived freezing in the Atlantic after the ship went down in Titanic. ("They didn't have anyone confirm his death and there was no funeral! I think he survived and found her and she kept it a secret!")

After a while I stopped arguing with her, although not only did I believe he was dead, I thought there was enough room on that door/raft that Rose could have saved him, but whatever. Pretty sure Claire believes in unicorns, too.

Honestly, I had no idea how we were such close friends, but we'd been together since grade school. Margot, the third member of our trio, had gone to private school up until ninth grade, when she finally convinced her parents that she couldn't catch New Moneyitis by attending public schools. We'd each gone to different colleges but had moved back to the area after grad school, and we had standing GNO dates every week.

I waited the five minutes and called Claire, claiming to be her mother with an emergency at home. "I'll be right there, Mom," she promised in an unnaturally loud voice. "Fifteen minutes at most. Don't move."

We hung up, and she called me from the car ten minutes later. "Thanks. I was dying."

"Good thing you drove yourself." I carried my empty plate and glass into the kitchen and set them in the sink.

"Always. Especially this time. I had a feeling."

"What went wrong?"

"He spent the first thirty minutes of our date talking about his ex. He was in tears by the time my second glass of wine arrived. I took my entrée to go."

"What is it?"

"Veal piccata."

"Nice. Why is he even dating if he's not over his ex?"

"Who knows?" She sighed. "He was sort of cute, though. Great hair. It's a bummer. All the good ones are taken, I swear. Or gay. Or both."

"Speaking of cute, you'll never guess who just moved in downstairs." I turned around and leaned back against the sink, eyeing the fridge where he near-kissed me.

"Who?"

"Quinn Rusek." I lowered my voice. I didn't want him to hear me talking about him.

"*Quinn Rusek* just moved in downstairs from you? *Why*?"

"Because my brother told him he could."

"Your brother," she said wistfully. "A perfect example of cute, taken, and gay."

"We are talking about *me*," I reminded her peevishly. "And I have not heard the proper amount of outrage from you on my behalf that my cute, gay, and taken brother is subjecting me to this cruel and unusual punishment!"

"I'm sorry. It *is* cruel and unusual. What's he doing here?"

I filled her in on the details while I rinsed my dishes, put them in the dishwasher, and hunted around in my pantry for something sweet. "And then when I saw him, he had the nerve to act like nothing was wrong. Like he hadn't been such an asshole to me that night."

"Well, it *was* ten years ago, Jaims."

"That doesn't matter! My humiliation is still fresh! It rose right to the surface the moment he brought up the thing I said."

She gasped. "The 'I love you' thing?"

Spying a can of Duncan Hines frosting at the back, I pulled it out, took off the cap, and peeled back the foil lid. "Yes. Turns out he still remembers that. I'd been hoping he forgot." I dragged a finger through the thick chocolate sludge and licked it off. "It was so horrible. He teased me about it. Made me feel seventeen years old and ridiculous again."

"What an asshole," she said, finally giving me what I wanted. "How did he look?"

I groaned and dug back into the frosting. "Good. Too good. You can't trust people that good-looking. He's probably an alien or something. He's just here trying to charm women back to the mother ship to breed his ridiculously beautiful alien babies." I sucked the chocolate off my finger.

Claire laughed. "OK, don't follow him to any spaceships, but maybe you can try the whole bikini seduction again. Bet he'd go for you now."

"*Wrong*. He came up here, and I'm so stupid and gullible, I invited him in for a glass of wine. Talked about myself. Tried to get him to kiss me."

"Omigod! Why?"

I squeezed my eyes shut. "I have no idea. I swear to God, it came out of nowhere! One minute I'm telling him I won't go on a date with him, and the next, I'm puckering up! He's got some sort of weird spell on me or something!"

"Wait, he asked you for a date?"

"Yes. No. You know what? I don't even know." I stabbed the frosting. "He's so damn cagey, somehow I don't even know what he's saying. Plus I get distracted by his face." I shoved the frosting-coated finger in my mouth. "And his body."

"Dang. So did he kiss you?"

"Nope."

"Why not?"

"Who knows? To torment me? I mean…I thought he wanted to kiss me. He was flirting with me, I think."

"You couldn't tell?"

"No. And I hate when I can't read people. It makes it impossible to keep the upper hand."

"Ah," Claire said knowingly. "The old upper hand."

"I have to have it," I insisted, wondering how many calories were in a can of frosting and deciding not to look. Instead I put the cap back on and stuck it in the fridge.

"I know you do. You are the master of the upper hand."

"The mistress," I corrected, and the thought of myself as a dominatrix made me giggle. "I need a whip."

"Totally. Maybe you could tie him up and punish him for turning you down again."

"Ha! He would deserve it." I thought for a moment as I stared at the refrigerator where he'd pinned me without actually touching me. "Problem is, I think he's the upper hand type too."

"Why?"

"I don't know. I just feel like he's good at taking control, at getting people right where he wants them."

She laughed again. "And where does he want you?"

"He *says* he wants to be friends."

"Friends?"

"Friends. But fuck that. I'm not going to be his friend," I said stubbornly.

"OK."

"I'm going to ignore him until he goes away."

"Good plan. That always works when you have a crush on someone."

"I don't have a crush on him!"

"No, no. I'm sorry, sweetie. Of course you don't."

I sighed as I turned off the kitchen light and headed down the hall to my bedroom. "But I can't stop thinking about him. Why is that?"

"Well, what if it's fate? I mean, what if there's even an underlying reason he came back to town? What if it was his destiny to live in your house? What if he's your soul mate, your one tr—"

"Claire," I interrupted loudly. "Repeat after me. There is no such thing as a soul mate. Or destiny. Or one true love. I just want to bang him, not ride off into the sunset on his horse. And I'm annoyed he's not cooperating."

She clucked her tongue. "You have zero sense of romance."

"What's the point? Even in books, all great love stories end in tragedy. Why should real life be any different?"

Now it was Claire's turn to sigh. "You know what? I'm beginning to think you might be right."

It should have made me feel good that she'd finally agreed with me, that I was right, that I was good at my job—selling ideas to people—but somehow it didn't.

It took me a long time to fall asleep that night, imagining him beneath me. (And I do mean *right* beneath me.)

Even a realist has to dream sometimes.

CHAPTER SIX

Jaime

The next morning I heard the front door open and shut at an absurdly early hour for a Saturday. For one foggy moment, I was concerned about an intruder until I remembered Quinn. *I bet he gets up early and goes to the gym*, I thought, snuggling deeper under the covers. *Fuck that noise.*

But I couldn't get back to sleep. Instead, I lay there thinking about his sweaty body, muscles flexing, breathing hard, until I finally couldn't stand it, grabbed my vibrator, and got myself off.

Afterward, I craved him more than ever.

What the hell was I going to do?

My pride would not allow for a third attempt at seduction, not after I'd failed so miserably the first two times. What was wrong with him, anyway? Had I not made it clear that I don't want a boyfriend, but I do want sex? What kind of guy turns down an offer like that?

It got me thinking. Who was Quinn Rusek, anyway? Maybe there was more to him than meets the eye (not that there was anything wrong with what met the eye, mind you).

I needed to focus.

I needed to figure him out.

Then I needed a strategy to make him want me.

I'd get my fill of him—literally—and then he could be on his way. Out of my house, out of my head, out of my life.

Over the next ten days, I carefully avoided talking to Quinn while at the same time paying close attention to everything he did. I even made a list:

- **Works out early Tuesday, Thursday, Saturday mornings.**
- **Goes to class MWF mornings, must work out later those afternoons.**
- **Late classes Tuesday and Thursday evenings.**
- **Cooks his own dinners (have smelled Italian things, chicken things, possibly steak after getting home at night).**
- **Binge watches Game of Thrones and House of Cards.**
- **Takes out the trash and recycling bins (even mine) without being asked.**
- **Sings Beatles songs in the shower sometimes (fave might be Rocky Raccoon, voice not too bad).**

- **Wears size 12 shoe (left pair of boots in the hall to dry).**
- **Wears size 32/34 jeans (left pair of jeans in the dryer).**
- **Posts selfies to IG once a day (shirtless if inside, has perfected the Flynn Ryder smolder)**

Gradually a picture was emerging of Quinn as a polite tenant, fitness buff, good student, vainglorious photographer, and generally happy, well-adjusted person.

Who wasn't interested in me.

"I don't understand," I complained to Claire and Margot over martinis at our weekly Wednesday GNO. "He was all about me that first night he moved in, and he's ignored me ever since!"

"Wait a minute, you just said *you've* been trying to avoid *him* for the last ten days," Claire said, sipping her Cosmo. "How is that him ignoring you?"

"There have been plenty of nights where he must have heard me come in." I refused to let him off the hook. "He could have come up like he did the first time."

"Why would he? You told him you weren't attracted to him." Margot blinked at me. "You told him to keep his hands to himself, did you not?"

"I said *maybe* I wasn't attracted to him," I reminded her. "And that was only to get him to kiss me."

"You're being ridiculous," Claire said, shaking her head. "And you never get this way over a guy."

She was right. If I wanted someone, I went after him. If it was fun, maybe we'd make it work for a little while.

But Quinn wasn't playing fair!

"Tell me about it." I tipped back my dirty vodka martini. "Want to hear something *insane*? I have this list of things about him, stupid stuff that doesn't even matter and isn't helping me get him into bed. But I keep adding to it!"

"Oh my God, Jaime." Claire rolled her eyes. "Quit obsessing over getting him into bed. Just go talk to him. Hang out a little. You complained about him playing games, but right now you're just as bad."

I gaped at her. "Do you know me at all, Claire French? I don't want to *talk* to him. I'm not even sure I *like* him." That wasn't exactly true…Quinn did sort of amuse me, and I liked the way he'd taken care of his mom. He just knew how to push my buttons.

"Then forget him altogether," said Margot. "It's not like you want a relationship."

"Ew. No." I shuddered.

"OK, so go bang someone else if you have to," added Claire, "but maybe you should let this one go."

They were probably right, but I couldn't.

Once I get a craving like this, it has to be satisfied.

The next day was Thursday, and I took it off from work in order to get some things done—a dentist appointment, some shopping, monthly lunch with my mother. She asked me how my toast for Alex's wedding was coming along, and it stressed me out so badly that I'd come home, put on some pajamas, and uncorked the wine a little earlier than usual. But I figured the buzz might help the creative juices flow, so I justified it by sitting down at my computer with every intention of working on the toast.

Instead I stalked Quinn online.

Half a bottle of Bordeaux later, I was sneaking down the stairs with my wine glass in my hand. *If I'm going to stalk him, I might as well do it right.*

His door wasn't even locked.

It's like he wanted me to come in!

And besides, I wasn't going to steal anything—well, maybe some undies—I was just curious. Quinn was never home before nine on Thursdays, and I'd be in and out of there in five minutes. Ten, tops.

I don't think I need to tell you, it didn't exactly go as planned.

CHAPTER SEVEN

Quinn

What the hell? Had I left my door open?

I'd overslept this morning, and I'd heard we were going to get a ton of snow today, so I'd left in a rush, hoping to beat the bad weather. Maybe I'd neglected to pull the door all the way shut behind me.

Taking off my boots, I set them on the hallway mat and glanced up the stairs toward Jaime's apartment, but didn't see or hear anything.

Then I walked into my living room, and it hit me—the scent of her perfume.

In my apartment.

It was unmistakable, and by now, familiar. Sweet and fresh and floral. She smelled like a perfect spring day in the middle of winter, and it made me want her even more every time I smelled it lingering in the hall. But she was so stubborn, rushing past me every time I saw her, barely making eye contact, saying nothing more than hello and goodnight. If it weren't for those telltale blushes, I might think she'd been telling the truth that first night, and she really wasn't attracted to me at all. Just today, during my workout, I was thinking about trying again with her. For fuck's sake, we weren't kids anymore. Did we have to play games? Life was too short not to go for what you wanted, and I wanted her.

Had she been in here today?

I closed the door behind me, set down my bag, and walked back toward my bedroom. That's when I realized I could *still* smell her. Then I heard a noise coming from my room and walked into it just in time to hear a small sound of girlish terror and see the closet door being pulled halfway shut from the inside.

What the fuck was she doing in my closet?

And was that a half-empty wine glass on my nightstand? Had she snuck in here to snoop around, thinking I'd be at class? All classes had been canceled for the rest of the night because of the weather, so I was home early.

For a moment, I just stood there, trying to decide if I was flattered or irritated. I settled on mostly entertained, especially seeing as she was fucking trapped now.

(I know I said I was over the games, but this was just too good.)

What's the best way to play this?

She'd gone to all this trouble, so I should give her a good show, right?

Suddenly I had an idea, and it made me want to laugh so hard I had to back out of the room. In the hallway, I composed myself and then re-entered the room, making more noise this time. A hiccup and little thump against the closet door told me I was right about her location.

Suppressing the urge to just throw open the door and expose her drunk, snooping ass, I walked right by her into the bathroom, unzipped my pants, and drained the lizard for her listening pleasure. I grinned as I imagined the horrified look on her face.

Then I flushed, washed my hands, and started the next act.

"So. How about a hot shower, gorgeous?" I said loudly.

She hiccupped again. Then I heard some rustling around in there, and I was nervous she was going to expose herself to me before I had a chance to expose myself to her—and I mean *full exposure*. I wasn't shy in the least.

I whipped off my Henley and spoke again. "Yeah, I think getting hot, naked, and wet right now sounds like a good plan for a cold afternoon."

Out of the corner of my eye I saw the top of her head start to poke out of the closet, and I tossed my shirt her way.

She came out even farther.

"Fuck, this is gonna feel *good*," I said. Then I pulled off my T-shirt and flung it in her direction, delighted when it appeared to hit her in the face.

She darted backward into the closet like a mouse.

I smiled. *Come on out and play, little mouse.*

And she did—just in time to see me preening and posing in the mirror, flexing my muscles, stretching my limbs. I kissed each bicep just for show before sliding a hand down the front of my pants. My dick wasn't hard, and I didn't necessarily want it to get that way—yet—so instead of touching myself, I moved behind the bathroom door to get ready for the grand finale, wondering if she'd use the opportunity to escape. Betting she wouldn't.

I pulled off my jeans and tossed them out. Next, I yanked off my socks, but I left those on the bathroom floor. Finally, I took off my underwear and flung them out, dying to know if she was still there.

I covered my junk with both hands and kicked the door all the way open.

There she was. On her hands and knees—*I knew I could get her there*—mouth open, eyes wide.

She gasped.

"So," I said, barely able to contain my delight. "Now what?"

Her eyes raked over me from head to toe. She licked her lips. "Umf," she said.

"Use your words, sweet pea. What are you doing in my bedroom?"

She scrambled to her feet, which were bare. Her toenails were painted candy apple red, which was also the color of her cheeks. She wore black yoga pants that clung to her scrumptious legs and a long-sleeved, charcoal gray sweatshirt that hung off one bare shoulder and said NAMAST'AY IN BED on the front.

"Uh, sorry," she mumbled, fiddling with her braid. "I was looking—I thought I heard—nothing." She dropped her hands and exhaled. "Forget it. I'll leave." She backed up a couple steps, but I saw the way she couldn't take her eyes off my hands.

"Why are you leaving? Too chicken to stay?"

Her head snapped up, and she gave me a surprised look. "Chicken?"

"Well, yeah. You came down here to see something, didn't you?"

Her mouth fell open. Fuck, those lips. That chin. I wanted to do such bad things to her pretty face… My dick started to swell behind my hands.

"See something?" she repeated.

"Yes. Isn't that why you were spying on me from my closet?"

She puffed out her chest in outrage. "I wasn't trying to *spy* on you!"

"Oh no?"

"No. I was just—curious."

"Curious. I see. And does this satisfy your curiosity?" I stood tall and gave her my best selfie smolder, the one she hated.

She parked her hands on her hips. "OK. I'll play this game. No, my curiosity is not satisfied. I can see that much of you any time I want. All I have to do is get online."

"Hmm." I pretended to be vexed by that. "You're right. So now what?"

"Turn around," she said imperiously, like a queen ordering her jester to amuse her.

I cocked a brow at her. Then I turned to the side, which I really feel is the best angle for my butt. "How's that?"

She tipped her head to one side and studied me critically. "It's OK. But I'm gonna need more."

"More?"

"More." She twirled a finger in the air. "Could you turn to the back please?"

I faced away from her, feet apart, and took the opportunity to grin while she couldn't see my expression. "How's that? Better?" When she didn't answer, I looked back over one shoulder.

Her lower lip was caught between her teeth, and if I'm not mistaken, she was swaying a little, almost like she was woozy. Then she snapped out of it. "It's a pretty good ass. I'll give you that."

"Thank you."

"But I'm still curious."

"Oh no. Now it's my turn."

She looked surprised. "Your turn?"

"I'm curious too. Take off your shirt."

She laughed. "Not happening, my friend. You had your chance to see my bits and pieces. You turned me down."

"That was ten years ago."

"That was ten days ago in my kitchen, and you know it. I dangled no-strings sex, and you didn't take the bait."

"Maybe I don't want no-strings sex."

"Maybe I don't want you to see me naked."

"Chicken."

She gave me a dirty look. Then she grabbed her sweatshirt by the hem and whipped it over her head.

Oh, fuck.

I turned around and stared.

Her tits were just as perfect as I remembered them in that red bikini—maybe even more perfect. A little bigger, a little rounder, with mouth-watering caramel-colored nipples that begged to be tasted.

"And?" she said, sticking her hands on her hips again. "Satisfied?"

I swallowed hard. My eyes had to be bulging out of my head, and my dick was threatening to bust through my hands like a racehorse out of the gate. Her body was *luscious,* and I wanted to explore every curve and crevice.

Hell no, I wasn't satisfied. "Now your pants."

She gave me a look that said *I can't even with you*. "Really? My pants? You don't want to fuck me, but I have to take off my pants?"

"I never said I didn't want to fuck you."

She pretended to think, tapping her lips. "Hmmm. I guess it was implied when you walked out of my apartment without even kissing me."

"If you win the game, you can name your prize."

"Ha!" She threw her head back and laughed. Her throat was pale and slender and made me think of more bad things I could do to her. "You think I'll want to have sex with you as a *prize*? I'll play your little game, *Quinn Ryder*. I'm no chicken. But the size of your ego is staggering."

"That's not the only thing."

Another dirty look.

While she tugged off her pants, I took the opportunity to adjust myself, but the harder I got, the more difficult it was to conceal my dick with my hands.

"There." She straightened up and threw her pants aside.

My breath caught. She wore tight little shorts that sat low on her voluptuous hips, leopard print edged in black lace.

In my head, a lion roared.

"So," she said, her eyes full of mischief. "Now what?"

CHAPTER EIGHT

Jaime

He looked at me like he wanted to tear me apart. But he spoke calmly.

"Come closer."

I hesitated, then sauntered toward him. I had no idea what we were doing—he was so fucking unpredictable, it drove me nuts—but I was game for where this seemed to be heading.

He didn't need to know that, though.

I wanted him to suffer a little for the way he'd teased me. If he wanted me the way it appeared he did, why the hell hadn't he acted like it before?

Men. *So* annoying.

Was it any wonder I didn't want to deal with one on a daily basis?

"Here I am." We faced each other—a standoff. In my bare feet, my head was level with his chest. He had pert nipples the color of wine. My *favorite* color. "Shall we see who draws first?"

"Pretty sure I have the only weapon in this contest."

"So let's see it, big talker." I cocked my head. "Or are you chicken?"

He smiled—and dropped his hands.

I looked down—and gasped.

I couldn't help it. There it was, right in front of me, the Dick that Got Away. And it was big and hard and thick. It was one of those pretty ones, too, know what I mean? One of those tall, symmetrical ones planted in a manscaped yard? Figured that Quinn would have a perfect dick. It was probably magical too.

I was dying to play with it.

Lick it like a Popsicle. Suck it like a peppermint. Ride it like a pony.

But I wouldn't let on.

I met his eyes again, kept my cool. "Impressive."

"Thank you. Your turn."

I tapped my cheek with one finger. "Well, now, hold on. I have to think about this. If I don't drop my panties, you win. I think I need to know what's at stake here."

"Meaning?"

"What's your prize going to be?" I thought for sure he'd say something like a blowjob or butt stuff, so I was shocked when he answered in an entirely different way.

"A date with you."

I dropped my arms. "A what with me?"

"You heard me. If I win, you have to go out with me—and no sex on the first date."

"Are you fucking kidding me?"

He smiled. "Nope."

For fuck's sake, this was ridiculous. He had a massive erection right now! Why did he want to date me? Couldn't we just fuck like two normal adults without feelings? He was making this way too complicated.

I shoved my underwear down, kicked them off, and stood up. "I win," I announced.

"I don't know about that," he said, but his eyes were drinking me in, and his cock was jumping between us. "I think I'd call this a draw."

"So what do we do?" My breath was coming faster. Between the nearness of his naked body, the smell of his skin, and the way he was looking at me, I was about to lose control. Was this on or not?

He moved closer to me, so close my nipples grazed his chest, which sent bolts of pure lust straight between my legs. Moving my braid aside, he lowered his mouth to my shoulder and brushed it softly up the side of my neck. "What do you want for your prize?" he whispered in my ear.

I shivered. "You know what I want."

"Well then, maybe we can come to some sort of agreement…" His eyes flicked to the bed. "On this bargaining table here."

Oh, it was *on*.

I licked my lips and caressed the tip of his cock with my fingertips. "I'd like to open negotiations."

"Fuck." He grabbed me and threw me onto the bed, pinning my wrists over my head. His hips anchored mine, his erection trapped between us. "I can't think if you touch me like that."

I wrapped my legs around him, my heart pounding. "Thinking is overrated. What do you say we just feel our way through this?"

He crushed his lips to mine.

Finally. Fucking *finally*.

Ten years I'd waited for this kiss—and by the way, *hell yes*, it was worth the wait.

With my arms restrained above my head, I couldn't get my hands on him like I'd been wanting to, but I used my legs to pull him closer and lifted my hips against his. He kissed me hard and deep, his tongue stroking mine, his scruff rubbing against my chin.

As the kiss deepened, I felt my desire for him surging through my body like a hurricane, gathering force and speed and intensity. He moved over me, rolling his hips so his cock rubbed against me in just the right way, and I could barely contain my excitement. Bucking up beneath him, my body begged for more.

His mouth traveled down my neck to my chest, and I arched my back, anxious to feel his lips on my skin. My nipples tingled and hardened, and I cried out when he sucked on one, then the other, taking the tight little peak between his teeth and biting lightly.

"Yes," I breathed. "Fuck yes. Bite me."

He groaned, swirling his tongue around the tip before closing his teeth around it once more and flicking it with his tongue. It felt so fucking good—that simultaneous sting of pain and flutter of pleasure, plus his cock rubbing against my clit—I could have come inside a minute.

I like sex fast and hard and focused on the finish—no lazy lovemaking. For me, the best part about sex is the *aggression* of it. The chase, the climb, the race for the prize.

I loved feeling like I couldn't wait to tear the clothes off a man and let our basest urges take over. It turned me on when a man wanted me so badly he turned almost violent with it, like an animal. Sometimes it made me want to tame him—take control and boss him all the way to the finish when *I* was ready (and I hadn't had any complaints so far…most guys are happy to come sooner rather than later). Other times, I enjoyed being ravaged and letting them go all alpha male on me. Either way, it was more about the act itself and the roles we played than the person—I didn't date that much and even when I did, somehow the best sex was never with those guys, anyway. Sexual chemistry was always better with men I kept at a personal distance.

But speaking of sexual chemistry.

I was burning up for Quinn Rusek, about to combust.

"Quinn," I panted. "I want you inside me. Now."

He pinched the nipple that wasn't caught between his teeth, making me gasp. "And do you think," he said, dragging his scruffy jaw down my belly, "you deserve to get your prize so quickly? After you behaved so badly today?" He clucked his tongue. "I don't think so, sweet pea. Turn over."

My pulse raced. "What?"

"You heard me." But instead of waiting for me to do it, he flipped me over himself and caught my legs between his knees.

"What is this? I thought we were negotiating."

"We'll get to that. But there's the little matter of your misdeed to deal with first." His hands covered my ass, kneading gently. "Are you sorry," he went on, his voice smooth and dripping with patience, "for sneaking into my apartment to spy on me?"

"I told you, I wasn't trying to spy, I was—*fuck*!"

He'd spanked me so hard my eyes watered, then held his hand over the stinging flesh.

"Are you sorry?" he asked again.

I gritted my teeth. "No."

Crack! The sound of his hand smacking my other ass cheek was as thrilling as the sting of it, and I loved the heat of his palm afterward.

"You are a very bad girl, even worse than I thought. Not only deceitful, but"—*smack!*—"fucking unrepentant as well." *Smack!*

My ass was *on fire*.

He grabbed a fistful of my hair and yanked my head up, leaning forward to speak low in my ear. "You are downright sinful."

Stars danced in front of my eyes. "Yes," I rasped, my jaw clenched.

He traced my ear with his tongue before biting my earlobe, his cock pressing against my hip. "What am I going to do with you?"

"Fuck me," I whispered.

His grip in my hair tightened, making me wince. "Oh yes, your prize."

"Do it," I hissed. *Enough playing around.*

He let go of my hair and slid his hand up the back of one thigh. "Spread your legs."

I widened my knees, and his hand slipped between my thighs, two fingers gliding easily inside me. I was so wet already it was nearly embarrassing, but his next words put me at ease.

"I love how wet you are for me," he whispered, pushing his fingers deeper. "I can't wait to get inside you one minute more." He got to his knees and flipped me onto my back again, this time lengthwise on the bed.

Leaning over to the side, he took a condom from the nightstand drawer and tore open the wrapper. I watched as he slid it on, mesmerized by the sight of him and practically trembling that *this* was about to happen.

Oh God, he's so gorgeous—look at that body, that face, that cock! You know, it seems really unfair that he got the looks and *the big dick. If I was a guy, I'd hate him. He's way too gorgeous to be real. Any minute now he's going to sparkle like a vampire or shapeshift into a bear.*

But a few seconds later he was stretching out over me, positioning himself between my legs.

Yes, I thought, sliding my hands down his back and over his perfect ass. *Give me what I want. Give it to me deep and hard and fast. Let me feel the way you want me—every thick, hot, hard inch of you. Let me see you lose control for me. Let me hear you.*

But he hesitated, barely inside me.

I wiggled impatiently. "Come on. Do it."

"Not so fast, sweet pea. There's something I want too, remember?"

Oh my God, was he fucking serious?

"Yes, yes, anything." I slapped at his butt. *Giddy-up, horsey. Let's do this.*

"Anything? Wow, you must really want this." He pulled out and teased my clit with the tip of his cock. "It is going to feel good, I promise you."

"Please, Quinn," I whimpered. "I need it. I've wanted this for so long."

"Me too, believe me." He gave me an inch. "But I want more than this from you."

"OK, yes," I said impatiently. "I'll go on a stupid date with you. Give me more."

I got another inch.

"Not just one date. You have to give me a fair chance."

"I will, I swear," I panted. "I'll even introduce you to my friends." What? Why the fuck did I say that?

Um, because you need to get laid. Just agree to whatever, you can worry about the details later.

"I'd love that." He slid deeper. "And how about being my date for Alex's wedding?"

Oh God, really? The wedding?

"Yes!" I cried out as finally gave me what I wanted, pushing so far I felt that sharp twinge deep within, the harbinger of a seriously fucking good orgasm.

Deliriously happy, I held him to me, delighted with the ragged breaths that escaped him as he moved, ecstatic that the fit was such perfection, and goddamn jubilant over the fact that not only did Quinn have a huge, hard cock but he knew what to do with it. I'd been with one or two guys in the past who had a nice big drill but no clue how to use it once it was plugged in.

Quinn was fucking magnificent.

Maybe it was because he worked out so much and had such a strong core, but he moved in ways I'd never experienced. His body undulated over mine in rippling waves, and he rocked into me with a tight, steady rhythm that had me spiraling toward my climax in record time, even for me. I moved beneath him, matching his strokes, our bodies becoming slick with sweat. My hands were everywhere—his back, his shoulders, his ass, his abs. I gasped and clawed and panted, racing toward the finish, and the more frantically I moved, the harder he fucked me.

"Yes," I rasped in his ear. "I love it hard like that. You're so *fucking* good, Quinn. Your cock feels *so fucking good*."

"Christ," he growled. "You're gonna make me come right now if you keep talking like that."

"Now!" I demanded, the tension in me coiled too tight to last any longer. "Fuck yes, do it!"

He cursed and drove into me even deeper, and everything inside me burst wide open. I held him tight to me as his body went plank stiff, color and light exploding behind my closed eyes as my pussy pulsed around his throbbing cock.

And didn't stop, didn't stop, didn't stop.

Every time I thought it was fading, I'd feel him twitch inside me once more, and my body would shudder with aftershocks.

"Jesus," he finally said.

My face was buried under his chest, my hands stuck to his ass. I peeled them off. "I think my handprints might be permanently seared on your butt."

"Well then, we'd be even."

I giggled.

"What's funny?"

"You. Spanking me like that."

"I can't be the first guy to do it. You're terribly naughty."

"You are the first, actually."

He propped himself up on his hands and looked down at me. How the fuck was his hair still perfect? "Really?"

"Really." My heartbeat, which had been in the process of slowing down, suddenly began to gallop again when I looked up at his face.

To be honest, I wasn't entirely comfortable with it.

"Let me up. I can't breathe," I said, wriggling beneath him.

"Sorry." He pulled out carefully and stood up. "I'll be right back."

While he was in the bathroom, I rolled off the bed, scooped up my clothes from the floor, and headed to the other bathroom. After cleaning up a little, I got dressed and congratulated myself on a job well done. The snooping mission had been a bit of a debacle, but since the big picture goal had always been to get him in bed, this felt like a victory to me.

A sweet, sticky victory.

Smiling, I went back into the bedroom, where Quinn was pulling his shirt over his head. At the sight of his bare stomach and chest, my stomach did this little fliparoo thing that annoyed me. *I need to get the hell out of here.*

Except wait...hadn't I promised him some sort of date or something? He hadn't meant tonight, had he? Crap. I didn't want to go anywhere with him tonight. Besides, the weather was awful.

"Look at all that snow," I said purposefully. Quinn had opened the blinds and although it was five o'clock and getting dark, I could see it coming down like mad. I walked over to the window and looked out over white-blanketed rooftops. "It's like a blizzard!"

"It is." Quinn came up behind me and nudged me in the back. "You better stay here tonight. The roads will be bad."

I smirked at him over my shoulder. "I live upstairs, remember?"

"Oh yeah."

I faced him. "Plus I don't do sleepovers. It's a rule."

His eyebrows went up. "There are rules?"

"Yes. But I agree the roads will be bad. Was your class canceled tonight or something?"

He grinned. "You know my schedule?"

"No." My cheeks started to tingle, which meant they were getting red. "Not your *whole* schedule." I moved around him, heading for the door. "I'm just very observant, and I've noticed when you come and go. I assumed it was a class."

He followed me out of his room. "Aha. Well, anyway, yes, it was canceled, so I'm in for the night. What about you? Did you take the day off?"

"Yes."

"And did you have any plans besides observing me in my natural habitat from your hidey hole in my closet?"

We'd reached the living room, and I whirled around to face him, hands on my hips. "For the last time, I wasn't spying!"

"OK, OK." He held up his hands in surrender. "Relax. I forgot—you were just curious."

"Exactly."

"So has your curiosity been satisfied, or would you like to know if I'm a good cook? I was thinking of making a pizza. Want to stay for dinner?"

I'd been planning on going up to my apartment—I wasn't one to linger after sex, unless a repeat performance was on the immediate horizon—but pizza sounded pretty good. Quickly I weighed my love for good pizza against my dislike for post-sex chatter. At that moment, my stomach growled, making the decision slightly easier. "OK. I'll stay for pizza." *For pizza, not for you, get it?*

He smiled. "Good. We can talk about our dates."

"Dates? As in plural? I thought it was just one."

"Well, there's the one first date. And then you said I could meet your friends, and then there's the wedding. So that's…" He counted on his fingers. "That's like three dates."

My eyelid twitched. "Do you have any wine?"

"No."

I moved for the door. "I'll be right back."

CHAPTER NINE

Quinn

While Jaime ran upstairs for a bottle of wine, I opened my laptop, put on some music, and started taking out the ingredients to make pizza. When I was working a lot, I never ate things like pizza, but it was something I really enjoyed making and eating now that I didn't have to be so strict about my diet. I even had a pizza peel and stone so I could do it right, and I'd grabbed my kitchen boxes out of storage last week so I could cook for myself again. Hotel living was horrible that way.

I pulled out yeast, flour, sugar, sea salt, and olive oil, setting them on the counter. Next, I found a mixing bowl and liquid measuring cup in a cupboard and ran the tap to warm up the water.

I couldn't stop smiling.

When was the last time I'd felt this happy? Before my mom died? I couldn't even remember. In general, I was an upbeat person who managed to find silver linings and didn't tend to fret over things I couldn't change, but it had been a while since I'd felt this good. Was it because I hadn't had sex in months and had broken a rare dry spell? Or was it her?

I thought about it as I whisked together the dry ingredients, then added the water and olive oil. I'd figured sex would be good with her—not only was she smoking hot and temperamental, but we'd wanted it for so long—what I hadn't counted on was how much fun it would be. How much I'd enjoy the challenge of her. How much I was hoping she'd want to do it again later tonight (and for fuck's sake, let me take some time with it…there were all sorts of ways I wanted to please her), and then again in the morning before she left for work.

Of course, that was before I knew about her No Sleepover rule. I'd have to work on that, but not tonight. She'd only turn me down, and I'd learned it was better to let her come looking for things.

Shaking my head, I laughed out loud thinking about the way I'd discovered her in the closet. It was so ridiculous. No complaints about where it went after that, though.

Jaime appeared in the kitchen doorway a few minutes later, a bottle of wine in her hands and an amused expression on her face. "From the sounds coming through the floor up there, I thought maybe the ghost of Prince was down here cooking me dinner."

"Alas. It's only me." I wiped my hands, crossed myself, and glanced skyward before turning the volume down. "Rest in peace, brother."

She opened a drawer and looked in. "Oh good, you do have a corkscrew," she said, pulling it out. "I couldn't remember if there was one here."

"How come so much stuff was left when the former tenant moved out?" I grabbed the biggest bowl I had and greased it with olive oil.

"She found a job in London, where her boyfriend was, and moved in with him, poor girl. She didn't want to take all this stuff since she knew she wouldn't need it, so we said it was OK to leave things." She uncorked the bottle and poured red wine into two glasses. "Once she was gone, I came in and cleaned and organized everything. I'm glad it worked out for you."

"Me too." I put the dough in the bowl and covered it with a towel. "I only had to take a few boxes from storage. God, I missed having a kitchen."

"So you're a good cook, huh?" she asked, handing me a glass.

I shrugged. "I'm OK. My mom taught me a few things growing up, and while she lived with me in L.A. we'd cook together when she felt up to it. Not that she ate much."

"Your mom was a great cook."

"She was." I took a drink. "Want to go sit on the couch? We need to let the dough rise for a while."

"OK." She followed me into the living room, where we settled next to each other on the couch. The curtains were open, and we both stared out at the snow for a moment.

"My mom actually liked winter," I said. "It's one of the reasons she never wanted to move away from here."

"You must miss her."

"Every day," I said. "I feel like I didn't get enough time with her, you know? It's like, when you're young, you can't wait to get away from home, and it's only later that you appreciate what your mom—or dad, or whoever raised you—did for you. Only later that you realize you should have listened closer, that you weren't done learning from them, that you still have questions about life."

She nodded, looking over at me. "What would you ask her now if you could?"

"More about her life—her childhood growing up in Hamtramck, what it was like being the daughter of immigrants, why she waited so long to get married and start a family. She was over forty when she had me, which I didn't ever think about before, probably because anything over twenty-five seemed fucking ancient anyway, so who really cared, but now I wonder about it. And when my father left her alone with a baby, what was that like for her?" I took another drink before going on. I'd never said these things out loud before, but it felt good, actually. "Was she angry? Hurt? Did she miss him? She never talked about him, and I had zero memories of him, of course, so it wasn't as if I missed him and asked questions. But what was he like? What made her fall in love with him?"

"I bet he was handsome." She said it nicely, possibly the only reference she'd ever made to my looks without making fun. "He must have been."

"Maybe. Guess we'll never know, since there are no pictures."

"Really? Are you sure about that?"

I shrugged. "None that I ever saw. I haven't gone through every single box in the attic, so I guess it's possible, but there wasn't anything in her bedroom or any other areas of the house. I don't think she was sentimental about him."

"Still. He was her husband and the father of her child. Hard to imagine not keeping any evidence of his existence, even if it was just for your sake." She put a hand on her chest. "I mean, I'm the least sentimental person I know, and I think I'd secret away at least one thing."

"Maybe I'll look around up there," I said, although I wasn't entirely sure I needed to see a picture of the man who'd abandoned my mother when there wasn't anything I wouldn't give to have her back. "I have to get all our stuff out of that house anyway. I've been putting it off, to be honest."

"Why's that?"

"Because there's so much up there, and the vast majority of it is useless old shit that should be thrown away, and it's hard to make myself do it."

"Want some help?" she offered. "Like I said, I'm not sentimental at all. I'll be ruthless. It could be one of our dates!"

I smiled at her. "That will not be one of our dates, but thanks for the offer. I might wait until my place is ready, anyway. That way I'd have a place to keep things if I wanted them."

"Alex said it will be ready in about a month?"

"Looking to get rid of me?" I gave her the side eye.

"Definitely."

"Well, I talked to the guy yesterday, and he told me three more weeks at least. Apparently there was something wrong with the electrical."

"Where is it?" she asked, tucking her legs underneath her.

I told her about the condo I'd chosen in a renovated skyscraper, its downtown location, and the awesome view I'd have of Comerica Park. "Although I'd rather watch from inside the park. I can't wait to go to a game."

"I noticed you wear a Tiger hat in a lot of your Instagram pics," she said, pouring herself more wine.

"Wow, you're really into me on Instagram, aren't you?" After elbowing her gently, I took the bottle from her and poured myself more too.

She elbowed me back. "Be nice. Or no dates."

"Oh, no. We already sealed the deal on those. You are stuck with me on several future occasions." I set the bottle down. "So do you want to tell me about these *rules*?" I made little air quotes around the word rules, so she'd know what I thought of them.

She sat up straight, ignoring my sarcasm. "No sleepovers. No excessive cuddling. No getting mad if I don't call or text back some days, no leaving things at my apartment, and no talking about *feelings*," she finished, rolling her eyes.

I nodded slowly, like I was taking it all in. "OK, define excessive. Like, if I do this…" I took her wine glass and set it on the table before grabbing her in a huge bear hug, leaning over, and smothering her face with my chest. "Is this excessive?"

"Stop it!" She tried to get out of my arms, but I was much bigger and stronger. "I can't even breathe!"

"So this is excessive? That's what you're saying?" I released her. "OK, good to know."

"God, you're such an asshole." She moved away from me on the couch and smoothed her hair.

"Just want to be clear." I picked up my wine glass. "That one seemed a little vague. The rest I think I've got—you want to sleep alone, you don't want to talk all the time, and you especially don't want to talk about feelings."

"Right."

"So those are all the things we can't do. What's on the yes list?"

She looked at me like I was crazy. "Sex. With a condom. For a limited time."

I nodded. "Got it. Sex with a condom but without feelings for a limited time. And what do you have against feelings exactly?"

"Not all feelings," she said defensively. "I *like* the guys I've been with. I just don't get all gaga over them because it doesn't last, and someone always gets hurt if they think it does."

"Always seems unduly harsh."

"I've never seen a truly happy marriage. Someone is always faking it or lying, or they've just settled into a comfortable pattern and don't have any motivation to change things."

"What about your parents' marriage?"

She made a face. "Please. I love my parents, but my dad has affairs and my mother looks the other way because she's too obsessed with her job to care. I think she's glad she doesn't have to pay that kind of attention to him anymore. That's not love."

I shrugged. "Love is different things to different people. Who are you to judge?"

She sat up straighter. "I'm not passing *judgment* on anybody, nor would I want anyone to pass judgment on me. I'm just saying that the notion of true, everlasting love is a crock of shit, and people who believe otherwise are temporarily deluding themselves, blinded by desire, or just plain foolish."

"You're right, you're not at all judgy."

She pinned me with her favorite dirty look before taking a big swallow of wine.

"What about Alex?" I challenged. "He's in love. Which one is he?"

She sighed, slumping against the back of the couch and staring into her glass. "Alex. I don't know."

"He and Nolan seem pretty in love and have been for a long time. Is that a crock of shit?"

"I will admit that Alex and Nolan have been together for years and seem genuinely passionate about each other. But I've just never seen it last *forever*, OK? And everyone expects it to. I'm just being truthful."

"Being truthful," I repeated. *It's being scared, is what it is.* But I couldn't say that to her. Not yet.

"Yes," she said stubbornly. "And no one can blame me for that."

"I'm curious." I put my arm on the back of the couch behind her. "How does it usually go when you give the rules to guys who are interested in you?"

She shrugged. "It goes fine. Some of them love it, actually. I think they're relieved to meet a woman who's not looking for a ring, just a good time and good manners. And if they don't love it, well then… They can move on."

"And what happens if you actually fall in love with one of these well-mannered commitment-phobes?"

She shook her head. "That will never happen. I'm smarter than that."

"But what if it did?" I pressed. "You can't control your feelings. Even smart people fall in love."

"Then I'd break up with him."

"What? Why?"

"Because it's gonna end sooner or later, and I might as well be the one to do it," she answered, as if it were obvious. "At least then I'd know when it was coming."

I shook my head. "Did you not get enough love as a child or something?"

"Oh, God." She gulped down the rest of her wine and set the glass down. "Look, I'm not saying love doesn't exist in some forms. I got plenty of love as a child. I love my family. I love my friends. I even love my life," she said, throwing a hand in the air.

"So it's just romantic love you think is doomed. Relationships."

"Eventually, yes."

"Don't you ever worry that you're closing yourself off from something a lot of people find joy in?"

"Nope. I have plenty of joy in my life. And I'm never hurt or disappointed."

"Are you happy?"

A look of surprise flitted across her face. "Happy?" she repeated, as if she'd never considered the question. "Sure, I guess so. Happy for now, anyway. But what else is there?"

"What do you mean?"

"Happiness is always a 'for now' thing, isn't it? People think, 'What do I want right now? Oh, this candy bar. Those shoes. That purse. Another piece of cake. Another piece of ass.'" She spanked her hip and gave me a coy smile. "But what we want changes over time, so what makes us happy changes over time."

I thought about that. "But don't you think it's possible to know that something or someone would *always* make you happy?"

"To know it for sure?" She thought for a second, her green eyes serious. "No. I don't. Do you?"

"Sure, I do. I mean, I've never experienced it for myself, but I have faith it exists."

She gave me a patronizing smile, as if I'd just told her I still believed in Santa Claus. "That's so cute."

"OK. I'll prove it."

"Prove what?"

"I'll show you that real love exists. I'll make you believe."

She stood up, her smile gone. "Really, that's not necessary."

"Scared to take the bet?"

"I'm not scared of anything! I just don't think there's any way to prove what you're saying."

"Chicken."

She started for the door. "I have to go upstairs for a minute."

I jumped off the couch and pushed the door closed when she tried to open it.

"Hey," she said, annoyed.

"Come on. Dare me to prove love is real."

She sighed, her expression pained. "No, Quinn, because you'll only do stupid things to try and make me fall for you, and I'll just get annoyed. The sex was so great today. This could be fun between us. Let's not ruin it."

I smiled. "I swear I will not do anything to make you fall for me—unless giving you a lot of orgasms is on that list. Because *that*, I'm going to do."

Her jaw dropped for a second, and then she gave me a flirty smile. "OK then. I dare you."

CHAPTER TEN

Jaime

I hurried up the stairs to my flat, buoyed by the phrase "giving you a lot of orgasms." Damn, that sounded good.

In fact, the more I thought about it, this whole setup was fantastic.

I had the hottest piece of ass ever living right downstairs, and he clearly understood my boundaries, even if he'd made fun of them.

Whatever—he'd thank me when it was time for him to move out and our little fling had run its course. A month was perfect! That's about as long as I liked my fuck flings to last anyway. Any longer and you were looking at *relationship* status, which was no good, because it led to expectations and resentment, the inevitable accusations and accompanying guilt, and finally the tragic ending.

Fuck that—I was saving us both from a stupid breakup fight that would make Owens family functions awkward for years to come if he stuck around here.

We'd have unattached, meaningless yet magnificent sex for a few weeks, and then get out of each other's way. It was perfect...as long as he didn't try to fuck it up. I was a little worried about those dates he wanted, because I wasn't totally convinced he wouldn't try to muddy the waters with hearts and flowers, which would completely kill my lady boner and ruin the fun.

And what about the whole "I can prove love exists" thing? Was he nuts? There was no way on Earth to prove that love either did or didn't exist, was there? What the hell was he going to do? For heaven's sake, look at the home he'd come from—his father had abandoned his mother when he was just a baby. What had that taught him about romantic love?

I didn't really have a reason for coming up to my flat, I'd just wanted to exit the conversation, but since I was up here, I used my own bathroom, changed underwear, and grabbed another bottle of red from the rack before heading back downstairs. Quinn was on the couch again, checking his phone. Was it possible he looked even more delicious since he'd said the thing about more orgasms? When would those begin? Before or after the homemade pizza?

Sex and pizza. God, my life is amazing right now.

"How's your harem today?" I went into the kitchen, peeked at the rising dough, and left the wine on the counter. "They like your early morning bathroom selfie with the bedhead hair?"

"They did, indeed. More than five thousand of them."

"Don't you ever feel weird about posting so many pictures of yourself?" I came back into the living room, noticing that he'd closed the curtains. I sat a little closer to him.

"Sometimes," he said, setting his phone on the table. "But I also get a lot of messages from people who say that my pictures inspire them to eat healthier or exercise more or set a fitness goal for themselves. Those are good things."

"Ah, so you're doing it for them," I teased, poking him in the side, "not for your own ego. It's purely altruistic, all the shirtless muscle pics."

He tackled me, throwing me onto my back and covering my body with his. "You're awful, you know that? Quit making fun of me, or I will excessively cuddle you to death."

"No, no, anything but that," I said, giggling. But I slipped my hands inside his shirt, rubbed them up and down the smooth, warm skin on his back.

He looked down at me with a glint in his eye. "Or maybe I'll tease you about the red bikini night, Miss I Don't Talk About Feelings."

I gasped. "You wouldn't."

"Oh no?"

Something clicked, and I saw it as an opportunity to derail. "Hey…you remember what I was wearing?"

"Of course I do." He kissed me, but it wasn't like the first time, in his room. This one was softer and sweeter, and allowed me to better appreciate the firm fullness of his lips, the taste of the wine on his tongue. He picked up his head. "Some things are unforgettable."

Feeling validated, I smiled bigger than I meant to. My heart beat faster than it was supposed to. My insides performed acrobatic feats they hadn't attempted in years.

A warning bell sounded in my head.

I ignored all of that and focused on the external things—the hardness of his cock between my legs, the friction making my clit tingle and ache, the solid weight of his body, his mouth sealed over mine, his tongue sliding inside—the safe things.

His kiss had me riled up fast, and I tugged at his jeans. "Wait," he said. "I'll be right back."

A minute later, he came back with his pants undone, condom already on, and peeled my pants and underwear off in one smooth motion. *Fuck yes.* I love a man who doesn't belabor the point. When there's a matter to be settled, let's settle it.

He sat back on the couch and I quickly straddled him, grabbing his shirt at the hem and lifting it over his head. Then I reached down and took his cock in my hand, rubbing the tip on my clit.

"You really are all business, aren't you?" His hands moved up my thighs and over my ass.

"Is that a complaint?"

"Nope." He groaned, his eyes closing, head tipping back, as I lowered myself onto his dick, inch by inch, until I was sitting on his legs. "Just an observation."

"Sometimes I mix business with pleasure," I said, taking a moment to appreciate how full with him I was, how deep he reached, how hard and thick he felt inside me. I loved being on top—loved the control and power it gave me, loved watching a guy fall apart beneath me. And Quinn was so beautiful, this view was like none I'd ever seen before. Fucking stellar. His bone structure was ridiculous.

Also his boner structure.

I circled my hips, smiling lazily at the way he dug his fingers into my skin. I took his head in my hands, curling my fingers into his hair, pinning those blue eyes with a look that said *I'm. Fucking. You. Get it?*

His lips looked so delicious I couldn't resist rubbing mine against them, less a kiss and more a tease. Then I took his bottom lip between my teeth, grinding against him a little faster. Fuck, I could get drunk on this feeling. It was a bigger kick and a higher high than from any other drug—I could feel my body making the climb, feel his taking me there.

His hands flexed on my ass, and he held me tightly against him as he started to thrust up inside me. I gasped, dropping my head back, each powerful jab taking me closer and closer to release. My lower body hummed and tightened, and I tilted my hips back to get the perfect angle—the base of his cock rubbing my clit and the tip of it hitting the magic spot. He moaned and cursed under ragged breaths, matching my rhythm perfectly.

At the precipice, I looked down at him, and the sight of his gorgeous face seized by the agony of pleasure sent me over the edge. I clawed his shoulders, crying out as I came long and hard.

My orgasm subsided just in time to feel the powerful, surging pulse of his, and even though I generally try *not* to look at a guy's O face since most are scary and beastlike, I'm happy to report that Quinn's O face is just as fucking hot as the rest of him. So hot that it rekindled the fire inside me, and I felt a second orgasm building.

"Oh God—Quinn." I chased it, riding it out on his throbbing cock as he held still, paralyzed by the intensity of his own climax.

When we were finally zapped of energy, I tried to get off him.

"Just a second." His hands squeezed the tops of my thighs. "Don't move yet."

I squirmed a little. "But I—"

"I'm not going to hug you or kiss you or talk about my feelings. I just want to enjoy my dick in you for ten more seconds, OK?" He pinched my ass. "Jeez."

"OK. I'll give you ten more seconds. But only because I came twice, and it's been a very long time since that's happened."

He looked happy. "Oh yeah? I like that. But you're probably going to tell me you did all the work."

"Not at all. I give credit where credit is due, and your dick deserves at *least* half the credit for those two orgasms."

"Half?"

I narrowed my eyes. "Maybe three quarters. Now can I get off?"

"Yes."

We cleaned up in separate bathrooms again, and I fought the sudden urge to come up with an excuse to leave. It was like an automatic trigger with me after an orgasm, some kind of fight-or-flight response—I always wanted to be alone.

Cut it out. Quinn gets you and gets what this is, or at least he appears to. If at any point tonight, you feel he's losing sight of the big picture, you can make an excuse and leave.

But he didn't, so I stayed.

I drank wine and watched Quinn make pizza, helped make a salad (even though he teased me by quizzing me on vegetables as if I didn't recognize them), and enjoyed the feeling of being warm and cozy inside his flat while the blizzard outside buried us in snow, the temperature dropping below zero.

We ate at the table—I impressed Quinn by gobbling two bowls of salad and scarfing three big slices of pizza—and talked about lots of different things, including places we'd been in the world and places we still wanted to visit. Quinn preferred Florence and I liked Rome; he liked cabins in the woods and I preferred a resort on the beach; but we both agreed Paris was a magical place and Marrakech was on our list of dream vacations.

"I wish my mom had gotten to travel more," Quinn said, leaning back in his chair. "There are so many places I'd have loved to take her just for the food."

"Did she ever go back to Poland?"

He shook his head. "Nope. I don't think she ever wanted to. Her parents didn't have great memories of it. But I'd like to go someday."

"Can you make any of the Polish food she used to make? Like those meatballs? Or the pierogies and sausage?"

He smiled. "I haven't yet, but you just let me know when you're in the mood for sausage and I will accommodate you."

"Very funny." After stacking our bowls and plates, I got up from the table, carried the dishes over to the sink, and began rinsing them.

"Don't worry about that. I'll do them." Quinn came in behind me with the leftover salad.

"I don't mind helping you. But after that, I should get going. I have to get up early for work, and the drive is going to be a bitch tomorrow with all this snow."

"Do you have to go to work? The roads will still be pretty bad." He covered the salad serving bowl with plastic wrap and stuck it in the fridge, while I loaded the plates and bowls into the dishwasher.

"Yeah, I do. I took today off to catch up on some things and got nothing done."

He poked me in the butt. "The allure of my closet was too strong."

"Oh, shut up." But I giggled as I rinsed our forks. "I still can't believe you caught me in there."

Shaking his head, he carried the leftover pizza into the kitchen and set it on the counter. "I can't either. It's a good story, anyway."

I gasped, whirling to face him with the silverware in my hand. "You can't tell anyone that story!"

"Why not? It's hilarious. And it has a great ending."

"What?" I shrieked. "No!"

"Well, then, I guess you'll just be that much more motivated to honor your agreement about our dates."

"That's blackmail," I sniffed. "You wouldn't."

He shrugged and smiled. "Guess we'll see."

I dumped the silverware into the dishwasher. "God, you're a smug bastard."

"And you're a dirty little snoop. Don't forget your wine glass in my bedroom."

I tossed my braid and went back to his room to get it, glancing over at the closet and bathroom with a smile. What a crazy day. The sight of his bed made my insides tighten, and for a second I was tempted to suggest another round.

What the fuck? You start breaking your own rules, he'll think you didn't mean what you said. He'll get stupid ideas.

Grabbing the glass off the nightstand, I went back to the kitchen doorway and poked my head in. I didn't want to get within touching range in case he was planning to bug me about staying over. I was strong, but not steely. Not when it came to him, at least. "Sure you don't want more help cleaning up?"

"I'm sure." He stuck the leftover pizza in the fridge. "Now get the hell out of here. Before your face makes me want to cuddle."

I grinned, ducking out of reach fast. "Night. Thanks for dinner."

"Night."

Upstairs, I got ready for bed and set my alarm extra early, since even getting my car out of the garage was going to be a pain in the ass. I'd probably have to shovel the driveway first. Shit, I should have called someone earlier about doing it. Oh well. I could shovel before getting in the shower and call it a workout, right? At least my car wasn't buried out there like Quinn's.

For a moment, I felt bad that I hadn't cleaned out the second garage space for him, a silly passive-aggressive way to let him know I wasn't happy with him here. I'd do it this weekend.

Switching off the lamp, I snuggled under my covers, curling into a ball. It really was cold tonight. I thought about Quinn in bed below me…bet his body was warm and toasty under the blankets. I felt a little tickle between my legs.

You stay in this bed, Jaime Owens. You had three orgasms today, and that is enough.

Sighing, I got out of bed and turned the heat up a little. My gas bill was probably going to spike this month, but my rules—and my pride—would be intact. I also took an extra blanket from the hall closet and threw it on top of my quilt.

Still, I shivered all night.

CHAPTER ELEVEN

Quinn

When I heard her door close upstairs, I texted Alex. **Hey. Who plows the driveway for you?**

Are you making a bad sexual joke?

I had to laugh. **No, asshole. We have a ton of snow and Jaime has to go to work in the morning.**

I know, I'm just fucking with you. Jaime takes care of it. She either calls or shovels it herself.

I'd been with Jaime all night—which I didn't think I should mention—and hadn't heard her call anyone. **Is there a shovel in the garage?**

Should be.

OK cool. Thanks.

I plugged my phone into the charger and got ready for bed, figuring if I didn't hear a snowplow in the morning, I'd get up and do it for her. I didn't have a garage door opener, but there was a key to the service door on the ring Alex had given me.

Fuck, it was cold. I'd have to get used to Michigan winters again. I never slept in clothes, but before I got into bed I put on some pajama pants (part of a set my mother gave me our last Christmas together) and a T-shirt. I got under the covers and stretched out on my back, hands behind my head, staring at the ceiling above me.

I could still smell her, and it made my cock start to stiffen.

She's up there right now. Was she asleep? Was she warm enough? On nights like this, with the snow coming down and icy wind whistling at the windows, was she ever tempted to break her rule and sleep with someone? Was she ever lonely? She was so different from any woman I'd ever been with. So many contradictions.

During sex, or when she wanted it, she was so fucking hot—the way she moved and talked and responded drove me crazy…she was liquid and molten one moment, fiery and explosive the next. But when it was over, that was it. She cooled off quicker than anyone I'd ever known. Let me be clear, I'd *never* had a woman tell me she wouldn't spend the night after I'd asked her to—*ever*—let alone make it sound like going out with me was akin to torture, somewhere between a full body wax and a root canal.

I wasn't sure which side of her made me want her more, the fire or the ice. The fire made our physical connection sizzle, but that ice made her more of a challenge, and it made me more anxious to get closer to her…not to break her, exactly, but maybe melt her a little. Get her to open up.

If it were anyone else, I might think she was just playing hard to get with her "rules," but I didn't think that of her. I mean, I thought the rules were bullshit and the whole Love Doesn't Exist thing was just a defense mechanism as well as a pre-emptive strike, but somehow I felt she guarded herself that closely, kept herself that distant, for a reason. She said it wasn't her family history, but then what? Had she had her heart broken in college? Or more recently? *There's no way it could be the thing with me, right?*

I wanted to talk to her some more about it, but dammit, I'd promised her we didn't have to talk about *feelings*.

What the fuck was the world coming to when a guy finally wanted to talk about feelings with a woman and she said no?

And why on earth had I bet her I could make her believe in love? What the hell was I going to do or say or show her to convince her it was real? I wasn't even sure I could recognize it in myself, let alone other people.

I lay there for what felt like hours, imagining her right above me, wishing she were curled up beside me, and wondering where the crack in her armor would be.

Her heart was in there somewhere—she'd given me little tastes of its sweetness in between all the teasing and rule-stating—like the chewy, gooey center in a hard candy lollipop.

I grinned.

Maybe I just had to lick my way to it.

CHAPTER TWELVE

Jaime

My alarm went off at six-thirty, and I groaned as I shut it off. Burying myself again beneath the covers, I whimpered about going outside in the frigid dark to shovel the driveway. Came up with a dozen reasons to just say *fuck work* and go back to sleep. Told myself that no reasonable person was getting to her office on time this morning.

But in the end, I dragged myself out of bed. When something needed to get done, I wasn't one to put it off.

Unless it was writing a toast to give at my brother's wedding. Then I was an expert at it. Just thinking about standing in front of two hundred people and talking about love and commitment made my eyelid twitch.

Relax. You still have a couple months.

Moving slowly, I pulled on thick socks, jeans and a sweater. Tugged on my ski pants, heaviest coat, a hat, scarf, and mittens. Finally, I stepped into my winter boots, laced them up a little tighter, and clomped down the stairs and out the side door to face the music. I hadn't even looked out the window yet because I didn't want to get too discouraged.

So I was shocked when I opened the door and saw that the job was nearly done. Done! As in someone had shoveled almost the entire driveway already! Perking up immediately, I heard a shovel scrape the cement and looked toward the street, where a figure in a puffy dark coat, wool hat, and gloves was banking snow on the berm.

Was it Quinn? It had to be, unless it was Alex, but I couldn't see Alex getting up at five just to come out here and dig out his sister who should have called the snow removal guys last night but was too busy fucking his friend.

I pulled the door shut behind me and walked down the driveway. The air was so cold it froze the insides of my nostrils as soon as I inhaled. Snow flurries fell softly, dusting the freshly cleared driveway.

"Hey," I called, my breath creating a silvery puff in the dark, icy air.

He turned around, and I saw the blue eyes right away. His smile hit me in the gut—so hard I nearly stumbled.

I didn't like it.

What the hell was he doing? He wasn't even parked in the garage, so he had to be shoveling for me. I appreciated the gesture, but this smelled like a boyfriend move. Was he fucking with me?

"Hey," he said back.

"What are you doing?"

"I'm clearing the driveway for you."

"Why?" I tried not to sound suspicious, but I think it came out that way, because he rolled his eyes.

"Because it seemed like a nice thing to do, and there wasn't a No Shoveling rule last night. But come to think of it, I *have* heard there is a high correlation between shoveling a woman's driveway and getting her pregnant, so would you like me to put it all back?"

Feeling foolish, I slapped him on the arm with my mitten-clad hand. "Sorry. I am, in fact, grateful, so thank you *very* much. I was dreading this."

"It is pretty cold," he admitted, going back to work.

"Can I help?"

"Nah, I'm just about done."

"How about some coffee? I could go make some."

"Actually, I'm heading to the gym in a few. My class was canceled for today."

Jesus. Only Quinn would voluntarily go work out on a morning like this. Especially after shoveling all that snow!

I looked at his SUV, which was a mound of white. "Can I at least brush off your car?"

"No, thanks. I'll get it."

Shivering, I wrapped my arms around my chest. "You have to let me do something nice for you."

He glanced at me. "What did you have in mind?"

"Blowjob?"

He grinned. "You're relentless, although that would warm me up nicely."

Me too, I thought, hopping from one foot to the other to keep my toes from going numb. *Maybe we could even do it in a hot shower. I could—*

"How about a drink after work?"

I stopped moving and gaped at him. "You're turning down a blowjob for a drink?"

"Can't I have both?" He stuck the shovel in the snowbank and gave me an imploring look. "It's *really* nippy out here."

I sighed, too cold to argue with him. "I suppose. Why don't we—oh wait. I'm supposed to meet my friends for dinner. It's Claire's birthday."

"What do you know, I happen to be free for dinner tonight," he said delightedly.

"Really. How fortuitous."

"I agree, and I will gladly accept your invitation to join you."

I cocked my head. "I'm not sure I offered one."

"Well, it's fucking ten below out here, Jaime. I can't stand around waiting for you to be polite. I'll die of hypothermia."

I groaned. "OK, OK. Fine. You can have dinner with us."

"Looking forward to it."

"I'll meet you here at seven," I said, backing up the driveway.

"Where are we going?"

"Antietam. It's nice but not crazy formal."

"I promise to look presentable and be ready on time." He clapped his leather-gloved hands together. "This is so exciting, Jaims! Our first date!"

Oh, God. I hurried into the house, wondering what the hell I'd just gotten myself into.

11

That afternoon, I called Margot to make sure it was OK that I was bringing Quinn.

"Hello?"

"Hi. I have a problem with tonight."

"Oh no, you can't come? Lindsay had to cancel because she has the flu, so it's just you, me, Claire, and Elyse."

"No, I can come, it's just—I'll have someone with me."

"You will? Who?"

I spoke through my teeth. "Quinn Rusek."

Silence.

Then laughter.

"It's not funny. He totally invited himself and I had to say yes."

"Why? Are you still trying to get him to bang you?"

"No, we did it already."

"What? When?"

"Yesterday."

"How'd you make that happen?"

"Uh, it's a long story." One I didn't necessarily want to share.

"So how was it?"

I kept my voice down, since I had a cubicle, not an office. "Amazing. Fun. Mind-blowing. So mind-blowing I agreed to go out with him three times."

She laughed again. "That's specific."

"Well, he kept making me promise more things in the heat of the moment," I complained, getting up from my desk. I'd take the rest of this call in the stairwell. "And I was in a weakened condition. He took advantage of me."

"What do you mean? Were you drunk or something?"

"Not exactly." I pushed open the stairwell door and waited for it to shut behind me. "Just…really, really turned on. He seriously does something to me. I don't know what it is. Well, I know partly. His face alone melts my panties, but once I saw the body, I was lost. And he's *really* good." I'd caught myself staring into space ten times already today, reliving yesterday's sexcapades in my head. My undies had been damp since 9 a.m.

"Damn. You're a mess over this guy."

"I'm not a mess over him. I'm simply—" I rolled my shoulders, trying to relax, unclench my insides. "I simply enjoy his company in very specific ways. And those ways don't involve dinner dates. That said, he's coming with me to dinner tonight."

"Well, I think it's nice he wants to do something other than bang. It's normal. And healthy. And maybe you'll actually enjoy the dates!"

"I don't want to enjoy the dates, Margot. Are you crazy?"

"Why not?"

I slapped a hand to my forehead. "Why not? Have I not explained this to you guys like a thousand times? Closeness kills the spark. I never end up having good sex with guys I date."

"That's because you don't want to."

"What? Why wouldn't I want to have good sex?"

"Because you don't want to have reasons to continue a relationship. Meh sex gives you a reason to get out. And great sex gives you a reason to avoid getting in."

"That is not true," I said. But my eyelid began to twitch. "Look, I was a psych major. I get it. Do I fear intimacy? Maybe. But it's fine, because I don't want it, OK? I fear giant lizards too, but that's also fine because I don't want a Komodo Dragon for a pet."

"Do you know how ridiculous you sound? You're the only woman I know who wouldn't be thrilled about this."

"I can't help the way I am."

She sighed. "Do you want me to see if Tripp can come? I originally told him it was girls only, but if you want another guy at the table, I can ask him."

I wrinkled my nose. Tripp was short for triplet—not that Margot's boyfriend was a multiple. But he was the third Percival Dodge Jewett in his family, so they went with Tripp for a nickname, since his grandfather had claimed Percy, and his father was called (not kidding) Deuce. Personally, I thought he looked more like a Percival than a Tripp, and Claire and I sometimes snickered about it. Not that he wasn't attractive in a clean-cut, Ivy League sort of way. But he wore boat shoes and pants with little whales on them, referred to his mother as Mummy, and used "summer" as a verb without a hint of irony. I wasn't sure Tripp's presence would help me tonight, although it might make me laugh.

"No, that's OK. At least we don't have to change the reservation if Lindsay isn't coming. Quinn can just take her place."

"Right. OK, see you there."

I ended the call and went back to work, where I was so busy that I lost track of time and was late getting home. Quinn's car was on the street when I pulled in the driveway, and I half expected him to accost me in the hallway with a corsage or something, but I didn't see him on my way up.

In my bedroom, I took off my work pants and blouse, quickly swapped my basic beige undergarments for something sexier, and changed into a short gray sweater dress and black knee-high boots. I didn't have much time left over for hair or makeup, but I plugged in my curling iron anyway, and while that heated up, I added more color to my cheeks, eyes, and lips. When the curling iron was hot, I curled a few random chunks of hair and pinned back the sides.

I was just adding earrings when Quinn knocked on my door. "Coming!" I yelled. After throwing my lipstick, phone, and wallet in a smaller purse, I went to let him in.

"Hi." He looked me over from head to toe. "Wow. You look gorgeous. Love the boots."

"Hi." It was all I could manage, my pulse had started racing so fast. He looked way too good, and he smelled fucking incredible. Did I really have to wait until after dinner to get my hands on him? I cleared my throat. "And thank you. You look nice, too." He wore dark jeans in a slim cut, a camel coat, and a blue scarf that matched his eyes. His scruff was trimmed, and his hair was parted on the side and combed back off his face.

"Thanks. You ready?"

"Give me one second." I went back to my bathroom and gave myself a quick spritz of perfume. When I came out, Quinn was holding my coat, and I slipped my arms into it. "Thanks."

While I was buttoning it, he put his face in the crook of my neck and inhaled. "Mmm, you smell good."

The feel of his lips on my throat sent a tingle down my spine, and I wriggled away from him. "I'm trying to button my coat."

"A thousand apologies. Is there a rule about sniffing you?"

I glared at him over my shoulder, and he held his gloved palms up. "Hey. I don't want to screw up our first date."

"You know, it wouldn't be our first date if you'd have asked me to your prom like I wanted you to." Oh, shit. I hadn't meant to say that.

It took him a moment—a terribly awkward moment—to respond. "I almost asked you, I swear to God."

"Oh, right." I rolled my eyes and pulled on my gloves before grabbing the bag with Claire's gift in it off the coffee table. "Let's go. You want to drive?"

"Yes. And I was serious," he said, following me out the door. "I did think about it."

"Who'd you take, anyway?" I asked as we walked down the stairs.

"Danica Newman."

"And was it fun?"

He shrugged, moving ahead of me to open the front door. "She gave an OK blowjob, I guess."

"God, you're a pig." I tossed my hair as I went by him, slipping into the cold dark. "Well, maybe later I'll show you the spectacular one you missed out on."

"Are you trying to make me hard already?" He adjusted himself before shutting the door. "Hey wait!"

He rushed past me as I was moving down the walk—which he'd also shoveled. "Let me pull in front of the driveway so you don't have to walk through the snow."

He jumped behind the wheel of his SUV and moved it forward a few feet, then left it running as he got out again.

"What are you doing?" I asked as he came around to the passenger side.

"I'm opening the door for you."

"Oh, Jesus. This isn't the prom, Quinn. All the chivalry really isn't necessary. I promise I'll let you take my dress off at midnight if you want to. In fact, we can skip the dance entirely."

"Stop taking the fun out of this," he said before shutting the passenger door. I buckled up as he moved around the car and got back in. "Now try to look happy." He leaned toward me and held up his phone in front of us.

"What the hell?" Before I knew it, he'd snapped the pic and was tucking his phone out of sight, inside his coat. "Gimme that."

Unbuckling my seat belt, I tried to get the phone but he fought me off.

"Feisty tonight, I like it," he said, laughing as he got me by the forearms. "But save some of that energy for later."

"If you post that picture, I'm never speaking to you again, let alone fucking you." I straightened up, smoothed my hair, and buckled in again.

"Right, because that always works for you. Now where am I going?"

I told him how to get to the restaurant, and we spent the fifteen-minute ride there talking about our respective proms and other social events we remembered from high school.

"Did you have a serious boyfriend back then?" he asked me. "I don't remember."

"Not really." *I spent my junior year mooning after you, asshole.* "My senior year I dated this one guy off and on, but we were headed to different schools, so we were never that serious. I did let him pop my cherry, though." I said this with a sly sideways glance at him.

"Oh yeah?" He didn't look at me, but I saw his hand tighten on the steering wheel. "And how was it?"

I shrugged. "It was fine. I wasn't super crazy about him, I sort of just wanted to get my virginity out of the way. I knew the first time wasn't going to be great for me. Seemed like it was for him, though."

"I'm sure it was." The hand in his lap balled into a fist.

I allowed myself a tiny smile of triumph. *If you wanted to be my first, Quinn Rusek, you should have done it while you had the chance.* "Too bad you rejected me back then. Maybe it could have been you."

"Oh, it would have been me."

"You sound awfully sure of yourself."

He laughed confidently, and some of my self-satisfaction melted away. "Not only am I sure it would have been me, I'm sure you would have enjoyed it more."

Now it was *my* hands curling into fists. Why the hell did I let him get to me? I practically spoon-fed him these opportunities! "Guess we'll never know. The restaurant is over there. Park on this side of the street."

He did as I instructed and turned off the car. "You're not mad, are you? I was just being truthful. That is what you like, isn't it? Laying everything out there up front?"

"Yes," I said stiffly.

"Good. Now look at me."

I did as he asked. "What?"

"I know I could have been your first. And we'd have had fun. But I also know that I wouldn't trade the memory of finding you in my closet yesterday and everything that came afterward for anything. Jaime at seventeen was tempting. Jaime at twenty-seven is fucking torrid."

I felt my cheeks getting warm, a smile tugging at my lips.

"And Quinn at eighteen was good," he went on, "if a little fast, but Quinn at twenty-eight is a hell of a lot better."

"I like it fast."

"I know you do. You're like a fucking cheetah." He tapped my nose. "But one of these days, you're going to let me take my time with you."

Tilting my head, I gave him a coy smile. "I'll trade you a date for a slow fuck."

He shook his head. "Uh-uh. No way. I'm getting all three dates, plus the blowjob you offered me, *and* the slow fuck."

"What am I, a goddamn buffet?" Irritated, I opened the door before he could play Boyfriend and come around to do it for me. "And by the way, I think this should count as two dates because you're getting to meet my friends already."

"Hmmm." Quinn's brow furrowed. "I'd consider that. On one condition."

"What?"

"I get to tell your friends about the snooping."

"No!"

"OK, then I get to be as romantic as I want tonight."

"What do you mean, *romantic*?" I made a face. "Like, touchy-feely at the table?"

"If I'm so inclined. And you can't squirm away or say anything about it. No blowing up the game."

I chewed on the thumb tip of my glove and thought it over. "If I agree to play along, you can't tell anyone about my snooping in your flat, ever."

He sucked air through his teeth. "Wow, that's harsh. I was really looking forward to telling that story, especially the part where I hit you in the face with my underwear."

"That wasn't your underwear, it was a shirt! Now do we have a deal or not? It's cold out here."

"That's because you opened the door."

"*Quinn.*"

"OK, fine. Deal." He held out his hand and I put mine in it to shake, but instead he tenderly kissed the back of it.

"Ew, what are you doing?" I pulled my hand away.

He looked at me with that stupid phony smolder. "God, I love getting romantic with you."

My eyelid twitched. "This is why. This is why I hate dating. All this sappy shit just drives me insane."

"I know," he said, laughing. "And I sort of care about your sanity, but it's going to be really fun to fuck with you in front of your friends. Now stay there."

I shook my head as he got out of the car, came around to my side, and opened the door all the way. "You *are* a sadist. I knew it."

"Well, I might be, but let's save that for later." He smiled devilishly and reached for my hand. "Come on, love bug. Can I call you love bug? What am I saying—of course I can! I can do anything I want tonight."

Oh my God.

I needed a cocktail.

Stat.

CHAPTER THIRTEEN

Quinn

I held onto her arm as we crossed the street.

"Seriously?" she said.

"Yes. It's dark and icy, and I can't have my love bug slipping and falling and hurting her precious little ass. I'll do that myself."

She sighed heavily. "Fine. Please just stop calling me love bug."

I granted her nothing but a smile. Inside the restaurant, she tried moving away from me and crossing her arms, but I didn't let her. Taking her hand, we approached the host together, who led us back to a corner booth where three women sat.

I recognized two of them as Claire and Margot, Jaime's friends from high school, but the third I didn't know. All three jaws dropped as we approached.

"Ladies," I said. "Thank you so much for letting me join you tonight. I know how much my sweet pea values her girl time. It's one of the first things she told me about herself." For effect, I kissed the back of Jaime's hand again while she threw knives at me with her eyes. Then I turned to the table and pulled off my gloves, sticking them in my pockets. "Quinn Rusek," I said, holding my hand out to the woman I didn't recognize, who was seated on the end.

"Elyse Martin." She shook it, her dark eyes wide. "Nice to meet you."

Next to her was Claire, whose curly red hair fell in ringlets over one shoulder. "Claire, good to see you again. And happy birthday."

"Thanks." She looked back and forth from me to Jaime, clearly confused. "Glad you could make it."

"And Margot, how are you?" I greeted the striking, willowy blonde next to Claire.

"Good." She regarded me with amusement in her eyes, almost like she was in on the joke, and I wondered if Jaime had spoken to her about me today.

"Have a seat," Claire said, gesturing across from her. "Please."

I turned to Jaime. "Can I take your coat, honeybun?"

She peeled off her gloves, angrily shoving them in her pockets. "Yes, thank you," she said through her teeth as she unbuttoned her coat.

I took it off her shoulders. "I'll be right back. You won't even miss me."

"You got that right," she muttered, plunking down in an empty chair across from her friends. "Is there a cocktail menu?"

Spying the coatracks in a room just beyond the bar, I hurried over and hung up Jaime's coat as well as my own. While I was out of sight, I posted the photo of Jaime and me in the car to my Instagram account, chuckling at how perfect it was. She had sort of a *what the fuck is that smell* expression on her face, whereas I was grinning ear to ear. *Off to a great start*, I captioned it. I gave it three hashtags: #sweetpea #firstdate #loveisreal.

Oh, God. She was going to kill me. This was way too much fun.

Slipping my phone back into my pocket, I went back to the table and took the seat next to Jaime, making a big deal about dragging the chair over to be closer to hers. She was reading the cocktail menu and scooted her chair farther away, but I just moved mine again. I looked across the table at her friends' faces, and every one of them was trying to figure out what the hell was going on.

A server appeared. "What can I get for you?"

"I'll take a Sazerac," Jaime answered.

"Good idea, snookums." I put my arm around her shoulders and nodded at the server. "She's always so smart. I'll have the same."

The server promised to be back shortly with our drinks, and I turned to the women across the table. "So catch me up, ladies. I haven't seen you in years." I kept my arm around Jaime and could just imagine the look on her face.

Margot cleared her throat. "Well, I work for my father, doing PR and special events for the philanthropic arm of his corporation."

"Nice. Are you married? Single?"

"Not married, but I've been dating my boyfriend Tripp for about three years."

"Oh, you have a boyfriend. That's wonderful." I squeezed Jaime's shoulder. "Isn't that wonderful, poopsie? They're in love, just like we are."

Jaime coughed and picked up her water.

"How did you and Tripp meet?" I asked.

"My father introduced us. Tripp's a lawyer at the firm my father employs." She was talking to me but staring at Jaime, who was obviously trying to do that telepathic thing women do with their eyes when they want to communicate something without words.

"And how about you, birthday girl?" I turned the charm on Claire, whose fair skin turned a little pink.

"I'm an elementary school art teacher," she said, picking up her cocktail.

"That's awesome. I'd love to be a teacher."

"Really?" Claire looked surprised. "I wouldn't have guessed that. I mean, you have such a successful modeling career."

The server showed up with our drinks, and Jaime grabbed for her glass like she was suffocating and it was an oxygen mask.

"That was never my long-term goal, though." I picked up my Sazerac and took a sip. "I'm still trying to decide what *is*, but every now and again I do think teaching is something I'd enjoy. I love kids."

"You do?" Elyse blinked at me.

"Oh, yeah. I was an only child, always jealous of people with lots of brothers and sisters. I hope I have a whole brood of them."

"Really?" Now Margot was staring at me too.

"Totally. Jaime and I want at least four or five, don't we, dumpling?"

"At least," she said flatly, clinging to her cocktail for dear life.

"How about you? Do you have children?" I asked Elyse.

"Not yet, but I'd like to someday. I should probably find someone to marry first, but that hasn't been too easy."

"I agree, it isn't easy," I said. "But you know what? You have to trust in fate."

"That's what I say too." Claire was wide-eyed. "You have to believe that someone is out there for you, and it's just a matter of time before you find each other."

"I agree, Claire. Take Jaime and me here." I gave her another squeeze, nearly spilling the drink she refused to put down, and kissed her cheek, which was difficult since she tried to lean away from me. "We weren't always the passionate couple you see before you today. Just two weeks ago, she was like a distant star, shining her light from afar, and I could only dream about her." I gestured grandly toward the ceiling.

"That's so beautiful," whispered Elyse.

Jaime snorted.

"And then fate stepped in. I needed a place to live, there was a vacant apartment right below hers…" I looked adoringly at Jaime, who gave me the stink eye. "She took one look at me and fell head over heels. Didn't you, gumdrop?" Her face was so full of fury, I couldn't resist rubbing my nose on hers in an Eskimo kiss.

"And of course," I went on as Jaime slunk lower in her chair, "one moment in this woman's presence and I knew—*I knew*—that it was meant to be. I mean, look at her! Who could resist the face of an angel?"

Jaime scowled like a scolded child, her lower lip protruding.

"She's practically glowing," said Margot, unable to keep from smiling. "Jaims, love suits you, it really does."

"So be patient," I said to Elyse. "Your true love might show up when you least expect him to."

The server came back and asked for our dinner orders, and I gave Jaime a little breathing space to quickly look over the menu while I did the same. But once we'd put in our requests, I put that arm right back where it was. When I was certain all eyes were on us, I leaned over and blew softly in her ear.

"Quinn, *darling*," she said, her tone shrill. "Would you mind? It's a little warm in here."

"I'm sorry, peaches, I just can't help myself when I'm around you. And I don't want you to catch a chill."

"Well, I'm fine. And I'd like a little more room, please." She looked so miserable, I eased up.

Sighing, I took my arm back but reached for her hand, holding it in my lap. "OK. This will do for now."

She sent me a murderous look but left her hand there, and the conversation turned to other things—how the holidays had stressed everyone out, trips planned for spring or summer, Claire's disastrous blind dates, Margot's new car, my mother's old house, Elyse's failure to keep her New Year's resolutions already. But Jaime stayed fairly quiet, and just after we'd ordered another round of drinks, I felt her hand moving over my crotch. My dick immediately responded.

What the hell was she doing?

I looked over at her and saw her smiling sweetly at Claire, who was describing some date she'd been on recently where the guy wouldn't stop talking about his ex.

Our chairs were close enough together and the restaurant dark enough that I didn't think anyone would notice, but damn it, sitting at this table with a raging boner would be really uncomfortable. And I could hardly adjust myself with her hand right there. Oh fuck, I was getting hard fast. She knew it, too; I could tell by the satisfied smile on her face.

I winced slightly as my cock bulged painfully against the seam of my jeans. I needed more room in a really bad way—and she wasn't letting up! The bigger it got, the firmer she rubbed it. Should I move her hand? Slide my chair away from her? Excuse myself from the table? I could, but I wasn't wearing a jacket, just a cashmere sweater over a button-down. The shirt was tucked into my pants, and the sweater wouldn't hide the obvious if I stood up.

Fuckfuckfuck, it felt good and terrible at the same time. She was being so naughty and it totally turned me on, but jizzing in my pants on our first date would not be cool, especially in front of her friends. I shifted in my chair, trying to adjust without being obvious.

"Quinnypoo," Jaime said suddenly, and *way* too syrupy, "would you be a lamb and go get my coat for me? I left something in the pocket I need."

I looked at her expression, which was both innocent and knowing at the same time. *Oh, you little devil. You did this on purpose.*

I didn't really want her friends to see the monstrous erection I had going, but I couldn't ignore the dare. And if I was going to take it, I was going to take it all the way.

I smiled at her. "Of course, kitten. Anything for you."

I stood up and made sure everyone got an eyeful. "Excuse me, ladies. I'll be right back."

On my way to the coatrack, I ducked into the bathroom and washed my hands, just for something to do while I counted to ten in Polish, my go-to task when I need to stop myself from coming too fast or get rid of an ill-timed hard-on.

Jeden, dwa, trzy… It worked. By the time I got to *dziesiec*, I was comfortable again.

I dried off my hands, adjusted my pants, and went to get Jaime's coat. There was probably nothing in her damn pocket, but whatever. I had to give her credit for fighting back a little. All the ridiculous names and overt affection had to be driving her nuts. Her friends must think we were crazy.

But it was a good time.

A perfect time.

CHAPTER FOURTEEN

Jaime

He did it.

That rat bastard stood up and showed everyone the big fat bulge in his pants like he was proud of it.

What were you expecting? The man has zero shame.

Still. It was kind of hilarious.

"Oh. My. God." Claire's entire face was pink. "Did you guys see what I saw?"

"If you mean the package on Quinn, um yes." Margot fanned her face.

"Package! It looked like a baby elephant was trying to escape!" Claire stage-whispered.

"I tried to look away and I couldn't," murmured Elyse. "It was almost hypnotic."

I started to giggle, bringing a hand to my mouth. I'd pulled the stunt to humiliate Quinn, but actually I was kind of glad my friends got a good look. There was a certain thrill in knowing that of all the women he could have, of all the women in the world obsessing over his image, I was the one next to him at dinner. I was the one with his arm on my shoulders. I was the one he wanted.

"OK, so what the hell is with you guys tonight?" Margot's eyes were wide as she shook her head. "Explain the love bug routine."

"Yeah, I thought you didn't even like him," said Claire. "And now you're in love?"

I rolled my eyes. "We are not in love. This is just another one of his little chicken games. He's trying to get me to crack because he knows how much I hate all the sappy love shit."

"So it's fake?" Elyse asked. She was Claire's friend from work, and we didn't know each other all that well, but she appeared devastated that Quinn's amorous gestures weren't real.

"Yes, it's fake." Our second round of drinks arrived, and I grabbed my wine for a sip. "But don't tell him I said that. He'll punish me."

"So, wait." Claire glanced over her shoulder to make sure he wasn't coming. "I'm confused. Did something happen between you guys since I saw you two days ago?"

"Yeah, they banged," said Margot.

"Twice," I added. "And it was phenomenal."

"God, you're so lucky," Elyse gushed. "He is *gorgeous*. And I don't care what you say, he adores you. That can't all be fake."

I shrugged. "He adores pushing my buttons, and he knows just how to do it. He always has."

"Maybe, but he's definitely hot in the pants for you." Claire laughed and picked up her drink in a toast. "That much is obvious. Well done. You got what you wanted."

Behind Margot, I saw Quinn approaching the table holding my coat. "Shhh," I said.

"Here you go, love muffin," he said, handing it to me. "I just got a call from my agent that I need to return, but I'm going to do it outside. I'll be right back." He leaned down to kiss my cheek.

My friends watched him go. (Actually, I'd bet every woman in the place watched him go. I hadn't missed the stares when we'd come in.) Someone at the table sighed.

"I agree with Elyse," Margot said. "He might be playing around tonight, but it's clear he likes you a lot. He wouldn't bother, otherwise."

"Totally," said Claire.

"Fine, we like each other." I laid my coat across my lap. "And we're attracted to each other. And we have fun together. But that doesn't mean we should date."

"Hello! That's exactly why you date someone!" Elyse blurted. "If I met a man who looked like that with a dick like that who wanted me the way he wants you, I'd be fucking over the moon!"

"Shhh," admonished Claire.

"He does have a nice dick," I admitted. "And he knows how to use it."

Elyse groaned. "I'm so jealous right now."

"What about his tongue?" Claire giggled into her Cosmo.

"Haven't gotten there yet," I said. "Maybe later. I promised him a blowjob for shoveling the driveway today."

"You guys sound just like my sister and her husband," said Elyse, while Claire and Margot nearly choked on their drinks. "I bet you get married."

"Oh, for fuck's sake. I don't want to marry him. I'm not sure I want to marry anybody." I stood up. "I'll be right back."

I walked past the bar to the racks and hung up my coat, and on my way back to the table, I saw Quinn talking to our server across the room. *What's he doing? Ordering more drinks?*

I went back and sat down, and he appeared at my side a moment later. He took his seat, putting that infernal arm around me again. "Sorry about that. Did you get what you needed from your coat?"

My cheeks burned. "Um, actually it wasn't in there."

"Oh really? What was it?"

"Um, a…lipstick."

"Of course." The look on his face told me he wasn't fooled, but I was saved by the appearance of our server with a tray of appetizers. *Thank God—surely he can't eat and smother me at the same time.*

"By the way, I thought you quit modeling," I said. "How come your agent is calling?"

"I did quit, sort of, but there were a few contracts I couldn't break. I have to go to New York next week for a few days."

"Oh."

And the weirdest thing happened. I realized that I was kind of sorry he was leaving for a few days…that I didn't really want him to go away…that I'd *miss* him.

No, it couldn't be that.

I'd miss the sex, that was all. Not the man. Things were just heating up between us, and his taking off now was like leaving a restaurant before the main course was served. I wouldn't miss him. I couldn't. My heart beat erratically, and the back of my neck felt prickly and hot.

He took his arm off me to eat.

And I didn't miss it. Not one little bit.

Whew.

My head was still in the right place.

It remained there until after coffee and dessert when we asked for the bill. "The meal's been taken care of," said our server. "Including gratuity. Thank you so much."

"What?" said Margot, who was pulling out her wallet.

We exchanged a look; she and I had been planning to split the bill.

I glanced at Quinn, who calmly sipped his coffee. His profile emphasized the sharp cut of his jaw, the smooth bridge of his nose, the stunning length of his lashes. My insides clenched. Was he really coming home with me tonight?

He caught me staring and winked, sending a little flutter through my belly.

"Quinn, did you do this?" Claire asked. "It's too much."

"Not at all. Happy birthday," he said. "It was my pleasure to be here, so thank *you*. This is the most fun I've had in a long time."

"I'm so glad Jaime invited you," she said warmly.

Quinn smiled boyishly at her. Finally, he'd dropped the act. "Actually, I think I invited myself. But Jaime had mercy on me." Those eyes looked my way. "She's got a big heart."

And things in my head started to shift.

I didn't say much on the way home, partly because I couldn't stop thinking about New York. Would there be female models there? Would he get hit on? Would he be propositioned at the hotel bar? Would he feel free to say yes?

Of course he would. Why wouldn't he? You have no claim on him, nor do you want one.

I didn't. I didn't want one. But truthfully, I felt a little ill thinking about him with someone else. And I couldn't wait to get him into my bed tonight—the unexpected jealousy had me even more anxious.

The other thing that had me reeling was the compliment he'd given me.

She's got a big heart.

It wasn't usually something people said of me. At work I was called things like sharp, creative, ambitious, good with a deadline. My family thought I was responsible and hardworking, which they appreciated, being career-focused themselves. My friends sometimes told me I was funny and loyal and trustworthy, and I'd heard from men I was sexy and fun. But I didn't think anyone had ever told me I had a big heart.

I never showed it to anyone.

"Tired, love bug?"

The term of endearment made me cringe. "Good grief. Please tell me the love bug show is over."

"OK, fine." He was quiet for a moment, then he started to laugh.

"What's so funny?"

"Your face."

I slapped his arm.

"I meant your face all night whenever I called you a name."

"You were ridiculous." But I giggled. "Snookums? Gumdrop? Where did you even come up with that shit?"

"I don't know. I guess you just inspired me."

"Please." I held up one hand. "I am not your snookums, nor do I want to be."

He sighed as he pulled into the driveway, lining up the passenger door with the sidewalk. "Aren't you ever worried you're going to hurt my feelings when you say that stuff to me?"

"Was that…" I sat up taller in the seat and leaned toward him, like I might have heard him wrong. "Was that the *F word* I just heard coming out of your mouth?"

He grinned, glancing over at me. "I guess it was."

"I thought we agreed not to talk about those things, but no, it is not my intent to hurt yours, so I'm sorry if I have."

He put the car in park. "Here, I'll let you out and then park on the street in case you need to get out in the morning."

"It's OK. I'm not going anywhere early." I put my hand on the door handle, but something stopped me from getting out of the car.

She's got a big heart.

"Quinn…have I? Hurt your feelings?"

He smiled. "No, I'm just having fun with you. But it's nice to know you care, buttercup."

"Blech. I'm getting out now. Are you coming in?"

"Yes."

I got out and waited on the sidewalk while he pulled up a little, leaving the car in the drive. Walking toward the house together, I felt his hand on my back, but I didn't complain.

When the front door was locked behind us, I turned off the hall light and started up the stairs, expecting him to follow.

He stayed where he was, so I stopped at the top and looked down at his silhouette in the dark. "Don't you want to come up?"

"I don't know."

My jaw dropped. "You don't *know*?"

"I'm not sure I'm in the mood."

Always a fucking game with him. "Felt like you were in the mood earlier."

He didn't say anything right away. Then, "You were a very bad girl at the table tonight."

"You deserved it."

"Your friends see what was going on?"

I nodded slowly.

"You wanted them to."

Damn him. "Maybe."

"Does it turn you on? Shaming me?" He started to move toward me then, slowly coming up the steps.

"Maybe." My heart pounded louder as he got closer, my knees trembling. When he was two stairs below me, our eyes were just about even. I was trying to read his in the dark when suddenly he grabbed the back of my hair, stepped onto the landing, and forced me to look up at him.

His breath was warm on my lips. "My turn."

CHAPTER FIFTEEN

Quinn

I kept my fist in her hair as I slowly walked her backward into her flat, using my free hand to open the door to her living room. Once it was shut behind me, I moved deeper into the dark room until we stood in front of the window. The curtains were pulled partway open, and some light from the street lamps spilled in through the glass.

I spoke softly but with an edge. "You're not going to talk unless I say so. You're not going to move unless I say so. You're not going to come unless I say so. Do you understand?"

"But—"

I pulled her hair so hard she gasped. "Do you?"

"Yes," she whispered.

"And when you speak, you will say only the words I tell you to say. When you move, you'll do only the things I tell you to do. When you come, you'll do it when, where, and how I want you to. Do you understand?"

She swallowed. "Yes."

"Good." I let go of her hair and unbuttoned my coat, sliding it off and tossing it aside. Backing away from her, I unwrapped my scarf and coiled it in my hands. "Take off your coat."

She worked her way down the buttons in the front and slipped it from her body, letting it fall at her feet.

"Now your dress."

Lifting it by the hem, she pulled it over her head and dropped it behind her.

Jesus fucking Christ, she was hot.

Framed by the partially opened drapes as if she were on a stage, her body was dimly lit from behind. She wore only the black boots with the high heels I'd admired earlier and some sort of strappy, black lace one-piece that made my cock jump up like it needed a better look.

I'd teased her about her pale skin, but she looked fucking luminous tonight. I loved the way her hair looked like ink spilling over her shoulders, the way the deep pink of her nipples peeked through the black lace, the way her chest rose and fell with her quick, short breaths.

"Turn around. Face the window."

"But the—"

"Do it," I seethed, "or we're done here."

Slowly, she turned to face the window. Her lingerie cut low on her back and high on her ass, and my hands ached to touch her. I knew she'd been about to tell me the curtains weren't closed and anyone could look up and see her, but it was late, the room was dark, and anyway, she deserved a little of this.

"How does it feel, being put on display like you did to me tonight?"

She didn't say anything.

"You can answer the question."

"I don't know," she said.

"Do you like it?"

"Yes and no."

"Why yes?"

"I like…being on display for you."

"And why no?"

"I feel embarrassed. Someone else might see in the window."

"You shouldn't feel embarrassed about your body. It's perfect. So perfect I'm not inclined to share it. Face me."

She turned around again, and I liked the way she held herself, spine straight, shoulders back, chin lifted, feet slightly apart. It was defensive but also a little aggressive, telling me I might be calling the shots, but they weren't anything she couldn't handle.

I wanted to test her on that.

"Get on your knees, Jaime."

She didn't do it right away, and there was a tense moment where I thought the game was over, but eventually she dropped onto one knee, then the other.

"Now your hands."

She put both hands on the carpet in front of her, and it reminded me of the way she'd crawled out of my closet to watch me get naked. *Well, darling, you're about to get that up-close-and-personal look you wanted.*

"Crawl to me."

She crept toward me at a snail's pace, her body swaying, her eyes on mine.

Yes.

Her movements were feline and provocative, but submissive too. My chest—and my pants—were fucking *tight*.

When she'd reached my feet, she stayed there, waiting for my next order.

"Closer, darling."

She moved in, sliding her hands up my legs, placing her palms on my thighs.

I rubbed my thumb along her lower lip, felt her panting against my hand. I edged my thumb between her teeth. "Such a pretty mouth. So soft and wet. And your tongue…" I slid my thumb in deeper, feeling her tongue glide along it. "I want my cock right here on your tongue. I want to feel your lips on it. I want to fuck that pretty little mouth and come down your throat. Would you like that?"

With my thumb in her mouth, she could only nod, but her eyes were wide and hungry. I took my hands off her. "Tell me you want those things. Exactly as I described them."

"I want your cock on my tongue," she said breathlessly. "I want it between my lips. I want you to fuck my mouth and come down my throat."

"Good. Unbuckle my belt." I stood still, my hands at my sides. "Take out my cock, but don't put your mouth on it."

She unbuttoned and unzipped my jeans, pushing everything down enough to get my dick free. Eagerly, she took it in both hands.

I stepped back. "Stand up."

She looked up at me, confused, but she did as I asked.

"Turn around."

When her back was to me, I took her wrists, crossed them, and tied them together with my scarf. "We won't be needing your hands for this."

With her hands bound at her lower back, I turned her to face me again, then pushed the top of her bodice beneath her tits, propping them up.

I lowered my head and teased one hard nipple with my tongue, just enough to make her writhe with impatience. She arched her back, thrusting her chest in my face.

I smiled and moved to the other one, circling it with the tip of my tongue but never taking it in my mouth. Reaching between her legs, I brushed one fingertip back and forth over her clit, just enough to elicit a strangled "Quinn!"

I shoved her back down on her knees.

"No talking." I took my dick in one hand and dragged it along her jaw, over that dimpled chin, and across her lips. "I'll touch you soon enough. Right now you're going to stay still and open your mouth for me."

She licked her lips and opened them over the head of my cock, and I felt my legs begin to hum, the pleasure starting to unfurl. Taking her head in my hands, I pushed in deeper, groaning at the hot, tight fit. I pulled out slowly and watched as she went after the tip with her tongue and tried to get it back in her mouth.

But I controlled everything, and I held her head

just far enough away from me that she couldn't get what she wanted.

Then I gave her a little, and she swirled her tongue around it, sucked it greedily.

I gave her some more, and she looked up at me, her eyes wild and desperate.

"You want it all?"

She nodded.

"Do you think you deserve it all?"

A little whimper of frustration.

"Are you ready to take it all?"

She nodded again, and I shoved my cock to the back of her throat, making her body twitch with the impact. I did it again and again, keeping my eyes on her to make sure she was OK, but sparing no force or depth.

I don't know how she kept breathing, but she never backed off, never struggled to get away, never looked at me with fear in her eyes.

Just hunger.

When I was close, I held her head still and paused for a moment with my cock buried in her mouth, her lips still a couple inches from the hilt. I almost wished her hands were free—what would she do with them? Wrap her fingers around the base? Grab my balls? Play with my ass? How dirty did she get?

"Oh, fuck."

The thought was enough to push me over the edge, and I came hard, yanking her head toward me as I thrust into her with short, rhythmic jabs that hit the back of her throat.

I watched it happen, and the sight of it made the

orgasm so intense I thought my legs might give out. My knees shook, my thigh muscles clenching and then weakening.

When it was done, I pulled out of her and she sat back on her heels, swallowing and then gasping for air.

God, she was fucking incredible.

And I wasn't about to let up.

"Your turn, darling," I said, putting myself back together and doing up my pants.

I helped her stand and pulled off my sweater, thinking quickly about how I wanted her. Well, I wanted her to sit on my face, but that gave her too much control over her orgasm, and I didn't want her to have any. I didn't want to untie her hands, either, so lying on her back would be tough.

That left her to stand—until she couldn't anymore.

I knelt in front of her. "Open your legs for me."

She widened her stance, and I ran my hands up the front of her thighs, over her lace-covered stomach. I took her breasts in my hands, kneading them gently as I brought my mouth just close enough to her pussy that she'd feel me breathing. "What do you want?" I asked her.

"I want to come," she said feverishly.

"More specific, please."

"I want you to make me come."

"How?" I twisted her nipples between my thumbs and fingers, and she swayed forward.

"With your tongue. I want you to make me come with your tongue."

"Good girl." I put my mouth on her over the

damp lace, kissing her lightly, stroking her with my tongue—soft, slow, leisurely strokes that made her body vibrate with impatience.

"Quinn, please," she begged. "Tell me what to say."

"Say you want more."

"I want more."

I took my hands off her breasts and moved the drenched swath of lace covering her pussy aside. "Like this?" I slipped my tongue low between her legs and dragged it up to the top in one firm sweep.

"Yes," she said, relief flooding her voice. "Yes."

I did it again, and this time I lingered at the top, teasing her open and fluttering the tip of my tongue across her swollen clit.

"More," she begged. "I still want more."

I gave her a little more pressure, then a little less. A little steadier rhythm, then slowed again. I changed my angle, fucked her with my tongue, but never stayed with one thing for too long. When I felt her legs begin to shake, I backed off.

"Please, Quinn. Don't stop," she panted. "You have me so crazy right now, I can't even see."

"Always in such a rush," I scolded. "I told you I wanted to taste you. Let me get my fill."

"Fuck yes," she said as I took her clit into my mouth and flicked it with my tongue. "Oh my God."

I slid two fingers inside her easily, pushing deep, and she moved against my hand, her cries high-pitched and plaintive. I felt her insides tightening around my fingers as the tension in her body reached the apex, and then she screamed my name as her legs buckled.

I caught her around her hips, feeling her clit throb inside my mouth as my cock surged with renewed vigor.

I have to get inside her.

The need was intense, almost violent, and disturbingly possessive. She wasn't mine by any means and didn't even want to be mine, but something in me demanded her, compelled me to claim her.

Jumping to my feet, I pulled her loose-limbed body over to the side of the couch and bent her forward over the arm. I undid my pants and shoved them to my knees, kicked her feet farther apart, and moved the black lace aside.

"Fuck," I growled. "I need a—"

"Just do it," she said, out of breath. "I need to feel you. Now."

I wasn't going to ask again. Guiding the tip of my cock to her entrance, I pushed inside her, both of us moaning at the slick, hot friction. *I'm fucking her without a condom. We're breaking a rule.* The realization that I'd scaled one of her walls made me crazy with lust for her, not like I needed any more motivation. But it felt like such a victory in this primal, testosterone-fueled way—like a prehistoric man taking out a wooly fucking mammoth.

Not that Jaime was a wooly mammoth, of course. (And I *probably* won't mention the analogy to her.)

On the contrary, her back was pale and smooth, and I put my hands on her shoulder blades as I drove into her, her skin warm and sticky.

Her perfume mixed with the scent of sex and

filled my head, made my blood run even hotter. Her bound hands at the small of her back reminded me that I'd intended to torture her tonight with slow sex, punish her a little for the way she refused to give me a chance, show her that sex wasn't always about the finish line and didn't have to be such a straight line. It was fun to take time to enjoy one another, play around, trade roles, exchange power. We were new together, but we were good together—I felt it, and I knew she did too. Her willingness to play along with these games told me that, sexually, we were totally compatible.

But the plan for a slow fuck?

Yeah, that went the way of the pterodactyl.

I grabbed her hair with one hand and wrapped my fingers around her crossed wrists with the other, aroused beyond my control by every sense—the sight of my cock pounding into her, the sound of her high-pitched cries and my caveman grunts, her smell, her taste in my mouth, the feel of her tight, wet pussy sliding over my dick—it was too much to bear.

I came so hard I felt the ground shaking beneath me, and I pulled her hair so hard she screamed—or maybe that was her own climax rocketing through her, rattling her bones, jarring her teeth.

I want you I want you I want you.

I couldn't stop thinking it, couldn't stop fucking her, couldn't bear the thought that she didn't want me, didn't want this, more than she wanted to protect herself.

I was inside her.

And I didn't want to leave.

CHAPTER SIXTEEN

Jaime

I can't breathe I can't breathe I can't breathe.

Something was crushing me. I saw nothing but silver, heard nothing but the cannon-fire of my heart.

What was this feeling? It was heavy yet weightless, scary yet soothing, unbidden yet welcome.

I couldn't focus, couldn't get control of my senses or emotions, couldn't remember where I was or how I'd gotten there.

Quinn. *Quinn.*

Quinn was here with me.

Quinn was inside me.

Yes. *Yes.* I wanted him there, loved the way his bare skin felt gliding over my walls. Loved the way he reached something so deep inside me it hurt. Loved the way my body slowly contracted around his in that mad, dizzying spiral until it couldn't take any more pleasure, exploded, and fell to pieces.

Falling to pieces.

I opened my eyes.

Whoa. Get ahold of yourself. Those were good orgasms, maybe the best you've ever had, but there's no need to fall apart, right? It's good chemistry, that's all.

Quinn was breathing hard behind me, hands braced on my back, which was probably why I felt like I couldn't breathe.

Yes, that was it. That was definitely it.

When I coughed, he took them off me.

"So," I said, peeking over my shoulder. "That was your slow fuck."

"That was *not* my slow fuck. I sort of lost control there." He started untying the scarf around my wrists. "Abandoned the plan."

"I'm all for that kind of detour. Think the neighborhood enjoyed the show?"

"Unless someone was standing right beneath your window when you undressed—"

"Or looking from their second-floor window across the street."

"Or that, of course—then they saw nothing. That's not to say the entire street didn't *hear* the show."

I smiled. "It was pretty loud."

"There. You're free." He tossed the scarf aside and helped me straighten up, then he slowly pulled out. "Free, but maybe a little messy. Can I get you a towel or something?"

"No, don't worry about it. Be right back." I hurried down the hall to my bedroom, shut the door, and went into the bathroom.

As I cleaned up, I started to panic. Not because

he hadn't worn a condom—I was on the pill and very good about taking it. I'd never had a scare.

Then again, I'd never fucked anyone without a condom. Ever.

My heart started to pound.

Why had I done it? What had made me so hungry for Quinn that I'd broken one of my ironclad rules? What did this mean?

Calm down. You were hungry for Quinn's dick, that's all. It's a nice one.

True. Maybe that was it.

But…but what about the big heart thing? And the New York thing? And the way we had such fun playing each other's little chicken games?

Exactly—playing. You're great playmates. Friends. And it's OK to miss your friends when they go away. And it's nice that he gave you a compliment, but for fuck's sake, don't be stupid. You don't have that big a heart, and even if you did, it's impenetrable.

I breathed a little easier.

Right. Quinn hadn't worn protection, but I had.

I always did.

I took off my boots and traded my lace romper for some flannel pants and a sweatshirt before going back out to the living room, where Quinn had turned on a lamp. He was completely dressed again but holding his coat and scarf, looking at some pictures I had framed on the mantle.

"When was that?" He gestured to a photo of Claire, Margot, and me in formal dresses.

I went and stood next to him, arms crossed over my chest. "Prom."

"Cute. And that one is Alex's college graduation?"

"Yeah, I didn't walk in mine."

"Why not?"

I shrugged. "I don't know. Too much fanfare, I guess? I'd earned the degree; that's what mattered to me, not the silly hat."

"You are truly a no-frills woman."

"I guess so."

He turned toward me. "Everything OK?"

"Yeah, why wouldn't it be?" I met his eyes, but I had to work *very* hard to keep my expression neutral. I didn't want him to think this was anything different than what I said it would be. That he was anything more to me. That this mattered.

Because it didn't. It couldn't.

"I don't know." He knitted his brows. "You seem a little off."

"Well, I'm not. I'm fine." *Cool as a cucumber.*

"OK." He looked at me a moment longer, trying to read me, and I willed my face to stay impassive.

"Maybe I'm tired," I said.

"Of course. I'll let you get some sleep." He leaned over to kiss me, and I gave him my cheek. At the brush of his stubble on my skin, my insides swirled a little, remembering the feel of it between my legs. He left his lips on my cheek a moment, then straightened up. "Night."

"Night," I said, walking toward the door. At this point I didn't trust myself to look him in the eye. I opened it and he walked out without another word.

After I closed it behind him, I stood there staring at the door, chewing on a thumbnail, hating myself for being so cold to him after such a nice night, but unable to handle my feelings.

The knock on the door startled me.

I took a deep breath before pulling it open.

"Was it too much for you?" Quinn asked, his blue eyes serious. "What I did?"

"Which part?"

"I don't know—any of it." He ran a hand through his hair. It still looked perfect. "The stuff at the restaurant. The window and the kneeling and the scarf. The broken rule."

God, Quinn. Don't look at me like that. I'm completely unable to handle my own feelings, let alone yours.

And I had no idea how to answer his question. The truth was complicated. If I considered each thing alone—the restaurant, the living room, the broken rule—the answer was no. None of that was too much for me. I'd had fun at the restaurant, despite the hideous romantic gestures and embarrassing nicknames. Sure, he'd made me squirm, but secretly I'd enjoyed being the sole focus of his attention.

I'd enjoyed his little shame game in the living room too, loved knowing that bossing me around like that was turning him on—it turned me on, too. Had he been a little rough? Yes. But rough I could handle. Gentle was a whole different ballgame.

The broken condom rule was more troublesome, but even that I could chalk up to simply getting carried away in the moment.

But put them all together, and this felt too all-consuming, too good from every angle, too *big* for me.

All I'd wanted was a little man candy, and he was offering me an entire meal.

"Say something," he implored. "I'm starting to feel bad."

I felt myself cracking. "Don't. Don't feel bad."

"I'm sorry if—"

"And don't apologize. For God's sake, Quinn. I had a great time tonight. I didn't do anything I didn't want to do or wouldn't do again."

"Really?" He looked relieved.

"Really." I wrinkled my nose. "Well, maybe not everything. I don't think I ever need to be called dumpling again."

He laughed. "I'll stick to love bug."

"Don't you dare."

We smiled at each other a moment, and even *I* felt reluctant to say goodnight.

"So does this mean you'll go on another date with me? Because that's what I want. Something more than just no-strings sex with you."

I winced. "I don't know, Quinn. I'm feeling a little…off kilter right now. I need to think through some things." *And you need to stop looking at me like that. Your face is totally incompatible with rational thought.*

"I understand. I'll let you get some sleep." He looked down at the scarf in his hands, then met my eyes again. "You know, if it makes you feel any better, you've got me off kilter, too."

"Jesus. Shouldn't one of us know what the fuck we're doing?"

"Oh, I know what I'm doing," he said with a wolfish grin. "It just took me by surprise. Night." He disappeared down the stairs, and I shut the door before I lost my mind completely and asked him to stay.

I didn't fall asleep until well after two in the morning. I was agitated and restless—I couldn't turn off my brain, and since my body was wired to it, neither could find any peace.

I was wrestling with thoughts and feelings that were completely foreign to me. Every admission was a cycle of disbelief, denial, and gradual (grudging) acceptance. Finally, I came to some conclusions.

I liked Quinn. Really liked him. It wasn't just his body or his face or even his dick. I mean, yes, he was sort of obnoxious about his selfies, and he liked making fun of me way too much, but I liked his sense of humor and his work ethic. I liked his manners. I liked the way he talked about his mom. I liked that he quit modeling to go back to school and find something he really wanted to do. I liked that he knew my family and understood where I came from. I even liked that he stood up to me—sort of.

What I didn't like was the way he had me doubting myself. It had been five years since I'd sworn off serious relationships, and in that five years I hadn't once regretted that decision. I'd stuck to my rules, had a good time, and never felt lonely, deprived, or hurt. The guys I'd dated casually here and there hadn't made an impact, exiting my life as easily as they'd entered it. They were nice guys—

smart, attractive, attentive, successful. But they didn't *do* anything to me.

There had been a few wild one-night stands and intense extended fuck flings, but not once did I consider anything more with any of them. That kind of passion just wasn't sustainable for more than a few weeks, and frankly, none of those guys were very interesting beyond the bedroom.

But my gut was telling me Quinn wasn't like anyone I'd ever been with before and didn't fit neatly into either category. He wasn't the dependable date with no spark, and he wasn't the guy I wanted to bang but not talk to.

I wanted to know him better. I wanted to talk to him. I wanted to listen to him talk about his past and his future, confide in him that I was terrified to make the stupid toast at Alex's wedding, admit that sometimes I was scared of ending up like my mother—married to my career, blind or complacent about my husband's affairs, unaffectionate and increasingly closed off, a woman with very few close friends and no visible excitement in her life.

I wanted to tell him how I felt guilty for thinking about her that way—after all, I'd lacked for nothing. Alex and I had grown up in a nice house in a great neighborhood, attended excellent schools, had plenty of clothes and food and all the extras—swimming pool, piano lessons, soccer teams, trips to Europe. Our parents attended concerts and games and conferences, praised our successes, gave us the occasional hard words, paid for our educations, supported our personal and professional decisions, and never pressured us to be anything we weren't.

That was love, wasn't it? I mean, my mother wasn't a hugger, never really said *I love you*, and had never seemed comfortable with my dad's attempts at affection, but that was just her. We knew we were loved, she was a perfectly fine mother, and my dad, for all his faults, was a good father.

But Alex didn't want to be like him, either.

I rolled over and punched my pillow a few times. Being an adult was fucking hard. There were all these complicated feelings to sort through. Wouldn't it be nice sometimes to have someone's ear while you did it? Even if that person didn't have any advice, just someone to make you feel like, no matter what, things were OK? That *you* were OK?

A friend could do that, but a friend wouldn't then give you an orgasm to turn OK into OMG.

Quinn Rusek could be my someone.

He could. It didn't have to mean that I was wrong about everlasting love being a myth—it could just mean I was willing to take a chance on getting closer to someone.

Quinn Rusek could be my someone.

He wanted to.

I just had to figure out how to let him without losing my bearings…or my heart.

I slept late Saturday morning, and by the time I got up and looked out the window, Quinn's car was gone. At the gym, I guessed. Ew, if we dated, would that mean I had to be all healthy and fit? Not that being fit was a bad goal, and I was pretty sure I belonged to a health club, but there was no way I could handle Quinn's level of dedication to his physical well-being. Maybe I could eat more vegetables or something.

I grabbed my phone and got back under the covers, intending to check my messages and email, but I couldn't resist checking out Quinn's Instagram first. God, he'd be so smug about that.

"That's right, I want to see your stupid hot face first thing this morning," I muttered as I typed his name into the search box. I tapped his profile picture, but it was *my* stupid face I saw on the screen, right next to his ridiculous grin. "Oh my God," I moaned. "I look like I just stepped in dog shit!"

Off to a great start was the caption. And then: #sweetpea #firstdate #loveisreal.

Three thousand people had liked it. And a bunch of them had commented with cute little emojis that turned my stomach. Other people had written things like **so jealous** or **who is that?????** or **why is she making that face, if I was her I'd be so happy.**

Quinn had commented, **That's my friend. She's making that face because she doesn't believe in love. I'm trying to make her believe.**

After that there were a bunch of **AWWWWW** and **So sweet!** and more disgustingly cutesy emojis and eye-roll-inducing ass-kissing and flattery.

Lower down, one merciful soul had written, **She's pretty**, and Quinn had written beneath that, **She's a lot more than that.**

I tossed the phone aside and flopped back onto my pillow.

But I was smiling.

CHAPTER SEVENTEEN

Quinn

I didn't call Jaime the next day—actually, I realized I didn't even have her number—and didn't knock on her door, either. She'd said she needed time to think about things, and I wanted her to have it.

On Saturday, after spending the morning at the gym, I used the afternoon to sift through a few more boxes in my mother's attic, forcing myself to fill a few garbage bags. I didn't find any photographs, but I did find her old recipe box, which I took with me. On my way home, I hit the grocery store and bought what I'd need to make a couple of her traditional Polish dishes.

After unloading the groceries, I stood still for a moment in the kitchen, listening for Jaime upstairs. I heard nothing and figured maybe she was out.

Or else she's hiding because you scared her.

I frowned, admitting to myself that could be the case. I hadn't gone easy on her last night. She'd said it wasn't too much, and she didn't strike me as the kind of woman who held her tongue when she had something to say, but I was a little uneasy about it anyway.

My phone vibrated in my pocket, and the screen showed a text from Alex.

Meet for a drink?

Sure, I replied.

We're near Eastern Market looking at some property. Detroit City Distillery in 45?

Sounds good.

I changed my shirt and shoes, checked my hair, and headed out. In the front hall I paused, nearly going up to knock on Jaime's door. If she was home, maybe she'd like to join us. It would be fun to hang out together again.

But I decided against it.

The next move felt like hers.

Alex greeted me with a hug, Nolan with a handshake, and I forced them to take a quick selfie with me, which I posted with the caption *Good friends, good whiskey* #DetroitCityDistillery. Actually Nolan was all for the pic, but Alex tried desperately to get out of posing, which reminded me of Jaime. They even looked alike—same fair skin, green eyes, and dark hair, although Alex was tall and thin with more angular features, whereas Jaime was petite and curvy.

Nolan, also tall and dark, wore tortoiseshell glasses and had a very short, neatly trimmed beard. I'd met him only once before, but I remembered him as outgoing, smart, and completely devoted to Alex. I thought he was a therapist of some kind, but I couldn't remember for sure.

"So how's it going at the house?" Alex asked once I'd ordered a drink. "Jaime treating you OK?"

"She's been great."

"Good." Alex looked relieved. "I was worried she was going to give you the ice princess routine."

"Oh, she tried," I said, laughing, "but she warmed up eventually." *And then she boiled right over.* "We actually had dinner together last night."

Alex's jaw dropped. "No way. Really?"

"Yeah. With some friends of hers."

"Wow." He picked up his drink. "After what she said to me the day you moved in, I thought she'd avoid you like the plague."

This should be good. "What'd she say?"

"Something along the lines of keeping her distance."

I shrugged. "What can I say, she can't resist me. Never could."

"So what's the history there?" Nolan asked, one eyebrow arched.

Alex and I exchanged a look. "Jaime had a crush on Quinn," he said. "Let's leave it at that."

"And does she still?" Nolan picked up his glass.

"She might," I hedged. Joking around was one thing, but I didn't want to sell her out. "We had a lot of fun last night. I'd like to take her out again—if that's cool with you, Alex." The server arrived with my drink, and I thanked him.

"I'm not the one you have to worry about." Alex sat back. "I'm totally cool with it, but Jaime hates dating."

I nodded. "She mentioned that. Several times."

"She's just stubborn," Nolan said, adjusting his glasses. "I know she loves her independence, but I think she needs someone who can call her on her bullshit."

"Oh?" I sipped my Old Fashioned.

"Totally."

"Nolan thinks he has Jaime all figured out," Alex said dryly.

"I do," he insisted. "I've got a bunch of friends and patients just like her—scared to get hurt, so they refuse to get close to anyone."

"I'm not sure that's it with her," I confided. "She said she's never really had a broken heart."

"Exactly. So why fix what isn't broken?" Nolan pressed. "She's gone all this time without being hurt, while probably watching women around her be disappointed by men they care about. Why should she bother?"

"Maybe," I said, glancing at Alex. "She did mention that your parents' marriage isn't her ideal."

Alex snorted, which totally reminded me of Jaime. "It's not anyone's ideal. But hey, it works for them, I suppose. They've been together thirty years."

"Has she ever mentioned wanting a family?" I asked, stirring the ice cubes around in my drink.

"Not that I can think of," Alex said. "But when Nolan and I have talked about adopting, she's supportive. I don't think she feels a family isn't a worthy goal; it's just romantic relationships she struggles with. I do agree with Nolan on one thing, though—I think fear plays a bigger role than she'd ever admit, but I also think she just enjoys being unreachable sometimes. She's my sister and I love her, but I think she gets off on being so cold."

"That's her armor," said Nolan. "She gets off on *wearing* it, being able to keep everyone out."

"You guys are going to adopt? I didn't know that. I think that's awesome." I changed the subject, not because I didn't like talking about Jaime, but I was starting to feel a little disloyal to her.

Only later when I was driving home did I realize that it was the first time I felt I owed Jaime my loyalty, rather than Alex.

On Sunday evening, I pulled my mom's recipe for pierogi with meat filling from the box. "Sorry about the store-bought dough, Ma," I said, glancing at the ceiling. "I'll make yours next time." To make it up to her, I played the Beatles on Spotify. Always her favorite.

Singing along, I peeled and sliced the vegetables, throwing them in with the meat to cook in the stock. Next, I peeled and cut up the onion, then fried it in butter until it was lightly browned. I never fried things in butter, and the smell reminded me so much of my mother, I felt myself choking up. Between the music and the aroma in my kitchen, it almost felt like she was there.

I took my time with the recipe, enjoying the feeling of closeness to my mother it brought me but lamenting again the fact that I hadn't thought to ask her more about her childhood. A song came on that she used to sing to me called "I Will," and I felt my chest get so tight I had to stop and take a few deep breaths.

I was composing myself over the bowl of meat filling when I heard a knock on the living room door. Wiping my hands on a towel, I turned down the music and went to answer it.

My pulse kicked up when I saw Jaime standing in the hall, dressed in jeans and a pink sweater, her hair in soft waves around her face. "Hi," I said, surprised but happy to see her. "Is the music too loud?"

"No, not at all. I like it." She grinned sheepishly. "And I smelled something delicious."

I laughed. "I hope it will be delicious. I found my mom's recipe box yesterday in the attic and decided to try her pierogies, but it's more complicated than I thought."

"Can I help?" She rose up on tiptoe, so cute and eager, I nearly kissed her on the nose.

"Sure. Come on in."

She followed me into the kitchen. "What can I do?"

"Let's see." Looking over the directions, I shook my head. "There's like eighteen steps in this recipe, even though the ingredients are simple. My mother made it look so easy."

"Well, put me to work," she said, pushing up her sleeves and washing her hands at the sink. "Can't promise my kitchen skills are anything close to your mom's, but if you have any easy jobs, I'm up for them."

"How about chopping the parsley?"

She nodded. "That I can do."

We finished the recipe together, laughing at our first batch of strangely shaped pierogies and cheering for our second batch, which more closely resembled my mother's. We boiled and then pan-fried them, just like she used to, and sprinkled them with cracked pepper. After a high-five for our efforts, we threw together a salad and quickly set the table.

"Let me grab some wine upstairs," she said once everything was ready. "Be right back."

A couple minutes later she came down with a large brown paper bag in her hand. Setting it on the kitchen counter, she unpacked a bottle of white wine, a silver bucket, and three glass jars with candles in them that I recognized from her coffee table upstairs. "I thought these would be nice on the table," she said, grouping them together like a centerpiece. "I think there's a lighter in the top drawer there. Can you grab it?"

"Sure." I found the lighter and lit the candles while she poured two glasses of wine, dumped ice in the bucket, stuck the wine bottle inside it, and set it on the table.

She placed a glass of wine by my plate and hers, then turned off the kitchen and dining room lights before sitting.

I returned the lighter to the drawer and sat down across from her. "Candlelight? A wine bucket? Who *are* you?" I teased. "This is way too romantic for the Jaime Owens I know."

She smiled and shrugged. "I like candlelight, what can I say? And I'm serious about my wine. I can't help it if it's romantic."

We filled our plates and dug in, praising our pierogies, even if somehow they didn't look or taste quite like my mom's.

I wondered about Jaime being here, if that meant she'd given any thought to my request for another date or my stating that I wanted more than just no-strings sex with her. After talking to Alex and Nolan last night, I wanted more than ever to gain her trust, assure her that I had no intention of hurting or disappointing her. But I didn't want to pressure her.

We ate mostly without talking, the music filling the space between us.

"You're quiet tonight," she remarked when we'd finished.

"Am I?"

"Yeah. Thinking about your mom?"

I nodded slowly. "The Beatles were her favorite, and she used to sing me some of these songs. I heard one earlier she used to sing at bedtime, and it really took me back."

"'Rocky Raccoon?'"

"No, but that's a great tune."

"I've heard you singing it in the shower," she confessed with a guilty smile.

"Such a creeper. Were you peeking in the bathroom window too?"

"No," she said, as if I'd greatly offended her. "I'm not that bad. Sheesh. So what was the song she used to sing to you at bedtime?"

"'I Will.' Do you know it?"

"No." She smiled. "Did it make you sleepy?"

"No, it brought back a nice memory, which made me happy, but I also felt a little sad. Not only for me because I miss her, but also because she won't be around to be a grandmother to my children, if I have any. Sing them to sleep that way. She'd have loved being a grandmother."

"You mean to our half dozen kids?" Her foot tapped mine under the table.

I laughed a little. "I forgot about those."

"Hopefully, we didn't get a jump on the first one Friday night."

My stomach hollowed. "What? I thought you said it was—"

"I'm kidding, it was fine. We're fine." She laughed. "Your face was so funny just now."

Picking up my wine glass, I took a generous swallow. "Yeah, I might like kids *eventually*. Not necessarily this year."

"I know, I was teasing." She focused on the wine in her glass as she swirled it. "But do you want to talk about Friday night?"

I studied her a moment. She looked curious, but not upset. "We broke a rule, didn't we?"

"We did. And while it was OK the one time, I don't think we should make a habit of breaking it."

"I agree."

She took a breath. "But there might be another rule we could break."

"The sleepover rule?" I asked hopefully.

"Not the sleepover rule. But the talking rule." Another deep breath as she met my eyes. "I want to talk."

"You mean, you want to talk about *feelings*?" I looked around the room. "What planet is this? Am I in some alternate reality?"

She threw her napkin at me. "Keep making fun and I'll *never* break the sleepover rule for you."

"I'm sorry," I said, retrieving her napkin from the floor and throwing it back at her. "Let's talk about feelings. What's up?"

"Well, I thought about what you said, about wanting more than just no-strings sex."

My heart beat quicker. "And?"

"And…" She lifted her shoulders. "I'd like to try. I'd like to be…closer to you."

I moved my chair back from the table. "Then you should definitely come sit on my lap."

Smiling, but in no particular rush, she got up and came around the table to stand in front of me. "Hi," she said shyly.

It was the most unsure of herself she'd ever looked, and it made me feel both aroused and protective. "Hi." I tugged at the sleeve of her sweater. "Come here, you." I pulled her onto my lap so that she straddled me, and she laughed softly.

Putting her arms around my neck, she rested her forehead against mine. "I don't know if I'm good at this."

"At what?"

"Strings."

I put my hands in her hair, gently this time. "Strings don't have to mean you owe me something specific. We don't need to put a label on this, Jaime. I just want it to mean something to you."

"It does," she said, kissing my lips. "You do."

"That's good enough for me." I kissed her back a little harder, tilting her head in my hands, tasting her with my tongue. My cock stirred between us, and she sighed as she circled her hips.

Her hands traveled down my chest and around my lower back, and I felt her start tugging my shirt from my jeans. But then she seemed to change her mind about undressing me and moved her hands back up my torso, leaving them on my chest. The kiss grew more intense, and I slid my mouth down her throat and one hand up her sweater.

When it closed over her breast, she whimpered a little. "I'm trying to go slow, I swear to God, Quinn. But when you touch me, I want to tear your clothes off."

I laughed. "Is that why you stopped before? You're trying to go slow?"

"Yes. But I'm so impatient." She moved her hips sinuously over my erection and whispered, "I can feel your cock beneath me, and I want it inside me so badly."

Oh, fuck. Moving my hands beneath her ass, I stood up and walked down the hall toward the bedroom with her legs wrapped around me, her lips setting my neck on fire. "We can slow down once we're naked—maybe. But at this point, I'll be lucky to make it to the bed."

She laughed throatily. "Wall, floor, bathroom sink—it all works for me. As long as it's you."

I reached the bed, set her on it, and we undressed each other frantically, her sitting and me standing. When she was completely bare, I pushed her knees apart, knelt down, and put my mouth on her, licking into her warm wetness as she lay back, hands in her hair. I did all the things I knew she liked, licking her slow and then fast, hard and then soft, sucking her clit. She came quickly, her legs across my shoulders, crying my name.

My cock was so hard it was almost painful, and I grabbed a condom from the drawer and rolled it on in record time.

Then I picked her up again. "So little," I said, easily holding her in place as she positioned me between her legs.

"So big," she murmured playfully as she slid down my shaft, her eyes locked on mine in the shadowy dark.

I turned and placed her back against the wall, feeling I showed great restraint in not fucking her right through the plaster, especially the way she was talking to me.

"You're unbelievable," she whispered in my ear as I drove inside her again and again. "You know how to make me come so hard—with your hands, your tongue, your cock. No one has ever made me feel this good."

I tried to last a little longer but felt powerless against the rushing current of desire inside me, which refused to slow down. Faster and harder I pounded into her, encouraged by the wetness of her pussy and the clawing of her nails and the loudness of her cries, telling me to *come, come, come…*

The orgasm spread throughout my body, every limb vibrating with pleasure as I went stiff and my cock throbbed. Afterward, my arms and legs weakened, and for a second I worried Jaime and I might both hit the floor.

Summoning my strength, I hitched her up a little higher before moving back to the bed and carefully setting her on her back. Expecting her to let go, I was surprised when she clung to me, arms around my neck, legs around my waist.

Braced on my hands, I looked down at her. "What are you doing?"

"I don't know," she said. "I just…don't want to let go yet."

"Then don't." I kissed her forehead. "Then don't."

CHAPTER EIGHTEEN

Jaime

Three days later, I met Claire and Margot for cocktails and oysters at Rockefeller's for our weekly GNO. We were sitting at the bar, listening to the live piano music and waiting for our drinks, when Claire pounded her fist like a gavel.

"OK, that's all the time I'm giving you. Tell us what's going on with you and Quinn."

"Well, we're...talking." I tucked my hair behind my ears.

"Just talking?" From the other side of Claire, Margot eyed me suspiciously.

"OK, talking and fucking," I conceded. "But talking is a big step for me."

Claire laughed and clapped her hands. "It is. We're very proud of you for talking."

"What are you talking *about*?" Margot asked as our martinis arrived—gin for Margot, Cosmo for Claire, vodka for me (dirty, of course).

"Different things." I sipped my drink. "We actually talk quite a bit about his mom. He misses her a lot. I think he likes talking about her with someone who knew her from before she got sick."

"That's sweet," said Margot.

"It is. He's actually much sweeter than I thought." I tried to say this casually, but I didn't miss the look my friends exchanged. "What?" I said in self-defense.

"Nothing, don't get your panties in a twist." Claire patted my shoulder. "We were saying as much to each other yesterday, that we think he's funny and sweet and would be really good for you if you'd give him a chance."

"Too bad he's so unattractive," Margot quipped.

"I know, right?" I shook my head. "I keep thinking about that. He could have anyone. What's wrong with him that he wants me?"

"Oh, shut the fuck up," said Claire, who rarely cursed. "You're hot, he's hot. There's chemistry. That's that."

I sipped my martini and listened to the pianist play "Let It Be," which we'd heard Sunday night as we made the pierogies. Quinn had sung along to it. "You know what? He'd like this place. I should bring him here sometime."

"You should," Margot said. "We could have dinner at the restaurant. Tripp and I, you and Quinn, Claire and—"

"Don't." Claire put up a hand. "No more set-ups. I will meet someone somewhere on my own; I can't handle the disappointment anymore. You guys go. I'll stay home with my Kindle and my cat. They never disappoint."

I tipped my head onto Claire's shoulder for a second, feeling sort of guilty that Quinn had landed in my lap after all this time. I hadn't even been looking to date someone—in fact, I'd been looking to avoid it. It didn't seem fair.

"So the talking is going well, then," Margot encouraged, her tone telling me she wanted more.

"Yes. I mean, it's only been three days, but…" I inhaled and exhaled. "I am cautiously optimistic I can handle what he wants from me at this point."

"Which is what?"

"He hasn't said, exactly, but I think it's just sex and conversation at the end of the day. He doesn't call or text me—actually, he hasn't even asked for my number, which is perfectly fine with me—and honestly, it's been me knocking on *his* door the last three nights." This last fact was a tad worrisome when I let myself think about it too much, but I told myself it was OK because A) sex with Quinn was really good, so who wouldn't knock on his door, and B) he was leaving for New York tomorrow for six days. We'd have a break then.

"I'm happy for you," Claire said, lifting her Cosmo to her lips. "Sex and conversation sounds great."

It was pretty great. So great I knocked on his door for the fourth night in a row when I got home from GNO, even though it was almost eleven.

He answered it wearing black athletic pants and no shirt. The bare chest and warm smile he gave me made my insides flutter, which was a feeling I was learning to appreciate.

"Hey," he said, his voice a little scratchy. "I thought it was girls' night."

Suddenly I noticed his apartment was dark behind him and realized he'd probably been in bed already, which got me all flustered. "It was, and I swear I was just going to go upstairs and go to bed because it's so late, but then I was thinking about you because I heard this song tonight that reminded me of you, and I thought about how I'd like to go to this place with you sometime because they play this old-school music, but I really shouldn't have knocked because it's so late and I know you have an early flight tomorrow, so I should let you go back to sleep, really sorry to wake you and—"

But then I couldn't babble anymore because he'd grabbed my head and pressed his lips to mine.

"I'm glad you're here." He moved backward, pulling me into his flat with his hands on either side of my face. "You should stay a while."

"Well," I mumbled against his lips, kicking the door shut behind me. "If you insist."

After a sweaty bout of me-on-top sex, we fell asleep, and I woke up around two. Silently, I crept out of bed and gathered my clothes, not bothering to put them all on, just my underwear and top. With the rest gathered in my arms, I couldn't resist giving Quinn a quick kiss on the shoulder.

"Hey," he said groggily. "You leaving?"

"Yeah," I whispered. "Sorry to wake you. Have a good trip, OK?"

"OK. Hey, can you leave your number for me?"

"Sure. I'll put it on the kitchen counter."

"Thanks." He was already drifting back to sleep when I left the room.

I missed him way more than I should have while he was gone, considering we'd only been "fucking and talking" for less than a week. But the house seemed so empty knowing that he wasn't there, which was ridiculous since I'd been living there for two months before that with no one in the downstairs flat.

He texted me every day, but it wasn't annoying. Just once or twice to say hi or send me a picture of something cool on the street or one of his ridiculous selfies. I confess, I stalked his Instagram relentlessly. One day he posted a pic of me I'd had no idea he'd taken—it was in his kitchen the day we made the pierogies. He'd snapped it from the side, catching me in profile, grinning happily as I tried to work with the misshapen lump of dough in my hands. *Miss this girl*, he'd captioned it.

There was just one hashtag: #sweetpea.

I rolled my eyes, but inside my chest, my heart was pounding.

Late Wednesday afternoon, the day he was scheduled to return, he called me. I let it ring a few times, even though I was totally anxious to hear his voice.

"Hello?"

"Hey, you."

"Hi." A stupid grin took over my mouth before I could help it, and I huddled down inside my cubicle.

"How's everything?"

"Good. How are you?"

"Great. Ready to get out of here. My flight gets in around five tonight. Can I take you out for dinner later?"

I almost said yes right away, but then I remembered standing Wednesday GNO. For a second I thought about faking an illness, but it would not be cool to bail on my girls for a guy. We just didn't do that. "I can't tonight. It's Wednesday."

"Oh, that's right. Girls' Night Out." He sounded more amused than disappointed. "How about tomorrow?"

"That works." But did that mean I wouldn't get to see him tonight?

"OK, I'll see you tomorrow, then. Have fun tonight."

"Thanks. Safe travels."

After the phone call, I found myself in a foul mood for no good reason. I was mad at myself for resenting GNO when I'd been the one in the past to insist we honor the date no matter what, and I was angry that Quinn hadn't sounded sad about not seeing me tonight. I'd missed that asshole. I actually couldn't wait to see him again, and I never felt like that about a guy. Did he not feel the same?

You see? This is why getting close to someone sucks. It's a constant guessing game in which it's impossible to keep the upper hand. Someone is always disappointed, and right now it's you. Get a fucking grip.

But I stayed grouchy through the rest of the work day and didn't even bother to go home and change before meeting Claire and Margot, because I didn't want to take the chance of running into him. First, I wanted him to think I didn't care that much about seeing him tonight, and second, I didn't trust myself not to ditch the girls and rip his clothes off the moment I saw his stupid face.

It was Margot's turn to pick the spot, and she chose Marais, an upscale French restaurant in Grosse Pointe with an elegant bar and lounge that wasn't exactly formal, but still likely to be full of crusty people like Tripp in coats and ties. I did like the cheese selection, though, which they wheeled out on a cart and gushed over before slicing portions onto a plate for you. I didn't give a shit about artisanal goats, but I had to admit it was all pretty tasty, served with bread and crackers and honey. They had a great wine list too.

I forgot all about my bad mood when I entered the bar and saw my friends sitting next to each other in a huge velvet booth, Margot visibly upset and Claire's hand on her arm.

"What's wrong?" I asked, sliding onto the bench across from them.

"It's nothing," Margot said, fighting for composure. "A fight with Tripp."

"About what?"

"You'll think it's dumb."

"Margot, no, I won't." I sat forward with my elbows on my knees, leaning toward her. "Talk to me."

She sniffed and pulled a handkerchief out of her purse. Claire and I exchanged a surreptitious smile—Margot was the only woman we knew who actually carried little white hankies in her purse, monogrammed with her initials. We sometimes teased her about stuff like that, but this wasn't the time.

"It's just—I thought we were really getting closer to an engagement. He's dropped hints here and there, and he knows it's what I want. He even asked me before Christmas about what sort of ring I'd like, so I thought maybe it would be a Christmas gift. But it wasn't."

"What did he get you again?" Claire asked.

"A Chanel bag and some earrings from Tiffany." Only Margot could make those gifts sound like a disappointment.

"How dare he," I teased, trying to make her smile.

She did, but barely. "I'm sorry, you guys. I sound like a spoiled brat, pouting because I didn't get exactly what I wanted when I wanted it."

"You're allowed to be disappointed. It's OK," Claire said, rubbing her shoulder. "You guys have been together for a while, and it's only natural for you to be excited about taking the next step."

God, Claire was such a nicer person than I was. All I could think was, *See? This is what happens when you give someone the power to make you happy—they can use it to let you down, too.*

"I just don't understand why he's dragging his feet," Margot went on, dabbing at her eyes. "He says he loves me. He's good to me. My family adores him; his family adores me. We come from the same world, have the same values, want the same things for our future."

Babies with little whale pajamas? I thought before I could help it.

"Well, what happened today?" Claire asked.

"It was last night, actually. I was being passive-aggressive and made a comment about being so old on my wedding day my dad would have to wheel me up the aisle, and he got defensive." Margot shook her head. "It was my fault. I shouldn't have poked at him."

"I don't think you were wrong to want to know where things stand, though, Margot," I told her. "He should be up front with you. But rather than hint around, can't you ask him flat out what he's thinking? Or tell him what you're thinking? That's not issuing an ultimatum. It's just being honest."

"But I'm scared," she said. "What if his answer isn't what I want to hear?"

I shook my head—this made no sense to me. Did she want to be deceived? "Why wouldn't you want to hear the truth?"

"Because it might hurt." She shrugged helplessly. "What if he doesn't want me to be his wife, and I just wasted the last three years of my life? What if he tells me I'm not the one? What if he doesn't think I'm good enough?"

"Then he'd be a total fucking idiot," I snapped, angry at the thought. "He'll never do better than you."

I wasn't even blowing smoke up her ass, it was totally true. Besides being smart, fun, and generous, Margot had the cool, aristocratic beauty of a Grace Kelly or a Hitchcock blonde. Sure, she'd grown up in a home with an elevator and a private French tutor, and she could be a bit clueless about the ninety-nine percent (the first day we met in ninth grade, she asked me in all earnestness where I boarded my horse), but she made fun of herself all the time. Sometimes she texted Claire and me things like, **When a sommelier tries to substitute the 88 Bordeaux for the 89. Please. #MargotProblems**

"I agree," Claire said firmly. "I think he does want to marry you, and he's just being a guy and putting off settling down. Try what Jaime said—talk to him openly about it."

Margot touched the hankie to her nose once more just as a waiter appeared at our table.

"What can I get you?" he asked.

"We'll have the *charcuterie* and *fromage*," said Margot, suddenly all poise and confidence, back straight. Letting a stranger see her upset was not her style. "And I'll have a glass of riesling."

But after we'd ordered and the waiter left, Margot's spine curled and she looked distraught again. "OK, I'll do it. I'll talk to him. Maybe this weekend."

"Good girl," I said. Personally, I thought Margot could do a hundred times better than Tripp and didn't understand the rush to get married anyway, but if she had her heart set on it, I'd support her. It was sad to me, though, that my gorgeous, classy, normally confident friend was letting a man dictate her self-worth.

That's what happens when women fall in love, though. They lose themselves. They lose perspective. They lose control over their own happiness.

Thank God I was smart enough to know it.

This arrangement with Quinn was really the best—I had all the perks of being in a couple and none of the heartache…as long as I kept my cool, I'd be OK.

For that reason, I did not check my phone even once to see if he'd texted.

I left Marais around ten, and his car was on the street when I arrived home. *Just go upstairs*, I told myself as I hurried up the walk. *Do not stop, do not knock, do not check your phone.*

I was unlocking the front door when he pulled it open. "Hey, you!" He threw his arms around me, pulling me inside, just like he had the day he moved in. "I saw you pull up. Did you get my text?"

"No," I said, disturbed by the way my pulse was racing. "When did you send it?"

"I don't know, maybe an hour ago. I kept telling myself not to bug you on girls' night, but then I couldn't resist." He took my wrists, tugged on them playfully. "I missed your face."

"Just my face?" I made a joke while I tried to get my bearings. If I let him know how happy I was to see him, to know that he'd texted, that was bad, right?

"Maybe I missed a few other parts of you."

"My brain, no doubt. My dazzling intellect. My sharp wit."

His eyes flicked left. "Yeah, let's go with that."

"Thanks."

"So would your intellect be available right now for, um, a consultation? See, I have this really hard…decision to make, and I think some heated *discussion* might help me…penetrate the issue. Gain some insight."

"Really. You have a hard *decision*."

He nodded. "So hard it's painful."

I smiled, feeling like I was on familiar ground again. Sex and games I could handle. "Well, I can't leave a friend with such a pressing problem. Want to come upstairs for a pow-wow? I'll try my best to wrap my *intellect* around your pre*dic*ament."

He slipped an arm around my waist, the other around my neck, and kissed me hard. "My predicament would be delighted to come upstairs, downstairs, or anywhere else you want it to."

"So, did you miss me? You haven't said." Quinn turned onto his side and propped his head on his elbow.

I was stretched out on my back next to him. We'd just finished round two, during which I'd executed the Wheelbarrow *and* the Reverse Cowgirl, so I was winded as hell. (We'd been so impatient for round one, it had happened on the stairs with zero finesse from either one of us, although I'd probably have a bruise on my tailbone tomorrow.)

"I may have thought about you once or twice," I teased.

"Once or twice, huh?"

I shrugged. "I don't want you to get a big head or anything."

He sat up. "Liar. You love when I get a big head. Be right back."

Giggling, I sat up and hit him with my pillow as he got out of bed. "Jerk."

He went into the guest bathroom like he always did, and I went into mine, thankful for the way he respected my need for space after sex. A lot of guys would have just used mine because it was closer. Quinn was considerate like that.

After using the bathroom, I took my pill and brushed my teeth. Believe it or not, I was actually contemplating asking him to stay the night, but when I came out of the bathroom, he wasn't back in my room. The hall light was on, so I threw on a T-shirt and went out to the living room, where a shirtless Quinn was tugging on his jeans.

"Had to find my pants," he said, his hair messy and flopping in his face. He pushed it back. "The rest of my clothes are still down there, but I brought yours up. They're on the couch."

"Thanks." I stood there for a second, arms crossed, not wanting him to leave but not certain asking him to stay was right, either.

"It's late, I better go. See you tomorrow." He came over to me and kissed my cheek, and a moment later, he was gone.

I turned off all the lights and got in bed, fighting disappointment and angry about it. What the hell was with me? Had I missed him that much? Had I really been about to ask him to stay?

Thank God he left, said a voice in my head. *You invite him once, he'll think he can do it all the time. You've got a nice thing going here. Don't ruin it.*

I turned onto my side and hugged my pillow.

The voice was right. We might be casually dating, but once the dates were over, he belonged in his bed, and I belonged in mine.

Even if it felt empty without him tonight.

CHAPTER NINETEEN

Jaime

"This is cruel. How am I supposed to get dressed for tonight if I don't know where we're going?" I had the phone tucked between my ear and shoulder as I surveyed my closet.

"It's not cruel. It's called a surprise."

"Are you tricking me? Is this some kind of ploy to get me to go see a sappy movie or something?"

We'd been dating for a month now, and so far I'd avoided having to sit through any insipid romantic comedies or sweeping dramatic epics where two people fall in love and then she dies. We stuck to dinner dates, outings like museums or shopping or a Red Wings game here and there, and we also stayed in a lot, making dinner together and watching TV. I'd learned to accept Quinn's desire to cuddle on the couch, and he'd perfected the art of "moderate cuddling" so that I didn't feel smothered to death.

Every time we went out, he snapped a pic of us and posted it with his goofy hashtags. Someone invariably commented, **Does she believe in love yet???**, and he'd reply, **I'll ask her**.

The answer was still no, usually accompanied by an eye roll or a sigh, and he'd have to report back with **Not yet** and a bunch of silly sad emojis. Sometimes he'd add something like, **Still trying!**

If he was still trying, he was being pretty underhanded about it, since other than the couch cuddling, he never tried to hold my hand or kiss me in public or talk about "where this was going." Occasionally, he tortured me with the horrible nicknames, but mostly he respected my rules.

Still, today was Valentine's Day, and I didn't entirely trust him not to get mushy.

"No, sunshine, it's not a ploy," he insisted. "Just wear whatever. You look great in everything and nothing."

"If I wear nothing, can we stay in tonight?" Because those were my favorite nights with Quinn. Sometimes we'd play games—we had this one where I was the landlady and I knocked on his door demanding the rent and he offered to be my slave to pay it off because he was a sexy starving artist living on a dream. Once he even painted my body with chocolate syrup and licked it off. (We went up to my place for that. I don't think I need to tell you that Quinn doesn't buy things like chocolate syrup.)

We had another game where he was the doctor making a house call and I was the proper Victorian lady besieged by *hysteria* (also known as sexual frustration) which could only be relieved by a *paroxysm* (also known as an orgasm) the doctor brought on with either his hand or my vibrator. (At first Quinn didn't believe me when I told him that this actually happened in history, and that vibrators were, in fact, invented by doctors whose hands were cramping up from flicking sexually frustrated Victorian beans all day long, but I swear to God it's true. Just another one of those fun facts stored up in my brain.)

"No." Quinn's voice was firm. "We are going out. Get dressed. And hurry up because I have something to show you."

"OK, fine. I'll be down in half an hour, you big bully."

He was laughing when I hung up.

I decided on a red pencil skirt with a bow at the top of the back slit, a black top, and just for fun, some leopard print heels. After pinning my hair into a loose knot off to one side, I put on my makeup, some earrings, and a little perfume. Before walking out the door, I grabbed my coat and the gift bag with Quinn's present in it—a Tigers T-shirt and a voucher from me for two tickets to opening day at Comerica Park. It wasn't like me to buy a guy a gift for Valentine's Day, but in my defense, I'd already been planning on doing the opening day thing for him because I knew how excited he was about the upcoming season, and Valentine's Day just *happened* to occur right around the time I had the idea.

Purely a coincidence.

Getting down the stairs in the heels and tight skirt was a bit of a challenge, especially holding my coat and the bag, but I managed to do it without popping stitches or turning an ankle. But when Quinn answered my knock, I went more than a little weak in the knees.

"Wow," I said. "It's kind of a shame it covers so much of your body, but you can wear the hell out of a suit." It was charcoal gray and hugged his shoulders, tapered smoothly at his trim waist, and showed a hint of his white sleeves beyond the cuff. He wore a dark blue tie my fingers itched to undo, and his hair was slicked back off his face, which showed off his eyes even more. "Are you sure we have to leave the house?"

"Not at all. Now that I see you in that skirt and those heels, I've got all kinds of better ideas." He leaned over and kissed my cheek. "You're stunning." Burying his face in my neck, he inhaled and then bit my throat. "I could eat you up."

Giggling, I squirmed away from him. "Don't muss me, or I won't go out with you tonight."

"How about later? Can I eat you later? We can play Little Red Riding Skirt and the Wolf." He leered at me.

"Definitely. What did you want to show me?"

"Show you?" His eyes were still hungrily taking me in.

"Yes, you said you had something to show me before we left."

"Oh, right!" He shook his head quickly. "You've got me all addled now. Let me get it."

He went down the hall to his bedroom. Pretty soon it wouldn't be his bedroom anymore—his condo would be ready first of March so he was moving in less than two weeks. We'd yet to break the

No Sleepover rule…as late as we stayed up sometimes, we always slept in our own beds. A few times I'd been tempted to ask him to stay, or to ask if he wanted *me* to stay, but sticking to that rule was one of the ways I kept myself convinced that what we were doing was OK. I wasn't losing sight of myself.

He appeared again, carrying what looked like a photograph in his hands. "I think you might have been right about my mom keeping a picture of my dad. I finally got through the last of the boxes in the attic, and this was in one of them, buried in a stack of old tax receipts and tax documents."

I gasped and set my coat and the gift bag on the couch before grabbing the picture from him, turning it right side up. "Oh my God. It's totally him."

The resemblance was uncanny. The man was older than Quinn but had the piercing blue eyes, the jawline, the sandy hair color. In the photograph, he was standing outside holding a new baby in his arms. From the angle of his head, it seemed like he may have been looking down at the baby and raised his eyes at the moment the picture was taken.

Quinn stood behind me, looking over my shoulder. "There's nothing written on the back, but…I think it must be him."

"I think so too. Is that you?" I pointed at the baby.

"Probably."

"Awww. Look at your cute little jammies. And your father was very handsome."

We stood looking at the photo another minute in silence before Quinn spoke. "It's funny, the way he's holding me—assuming it's me—he looks like he'd be a good dad."

He did, actually. Very natural and caring. "Maybe he was."

Quinn made a noise at the back of his throat. "For what, two years? Doesn't count. A good dad sticks around. A good *man* sticks around."

I nodded, not sure what to say. What difference did it make if your dad was handsome if he left you the way Quinn's had?

"I'll be a different kind of father."

My clothing felt tight all of a sudden. I cleared my throat and handed the picture back. "I'm sure you will be."

"Jaime," he said, "I—"

"Should we go?" I interrupted. I had no clue what he was about to say, but my gut was telling me I wouldn't be comfortable hearing it. The past month had been wonderful, and I didn't want anything to change. Staying focused on the present seemed important.

Exhaling, Quinn tossed the picture onto the coffee table and picked up my coat. "Yes. Let me help you with this."

"Oh, wait!" I scooped up the gift bag and held it out. "Your present."

He looked amused as he set down my coat. "My present? *You*, Nonbeliever of True Love, got me a present for Valentine's Day?"

"Well…" I drew the word out. "I got you a present, and I'm giving it to you on February fourteenth. Other than that, I don't think we should draw any dramatic conclusions."

"Of course." He pulled the shirt from the bag and held it up. "I love it! Thank you!"

"There's more," I said, feeling giddy despite myself.

He poked into the back and pulled out the slip of paper. As he read it, his eyes lit up. "Good for two tickets to Opening Day and a pregame blowjob."

I clapped my hands. "Do you like it?"

"Best. Gift. Ever," he said, kissing my cheek. "I can't fucking wait."

He picked up my coat, and I slipped into it. "You'll be in your new place by then," I said, buttoning up before pulling on my gloves.

"You'll finally be rid of me." He took his coat and scarf from the closet and put them on.

"Thank God. All the amazing sex has been *so* annoying."

"Oh, we'll still have amazing sex. We'll just have a new set of rooms to play in."

"Yay!" My heart thumped crazily. "I know I'm twenty-seven, but…I love playing."

"Me too. OK, playmate, let's go." He opened the door and gave me a little spank on the butt as I walked out, and I felt reassured that everything was OK.

He wouldn't tell me where we were headed, only that we had a reservation at eight. We were driving south on Woodward and had just crossed Forest when he slowed down and signaled, and I looked around excitedly.

Then I gasped. "The Whitney?"

He smiled as he turned into the driveway of the late nineteenth century mansion, a massive, three-storied, rose-colored granite monument reflecting the wealth of the lumber baron who'd built it in 1894.

I clapped my hands and squealed. "I love this place! My dad brought me to dinner here for my sixteenth birthday."

"So you've been here before. I wasn't sure." Quinn pulled up at Valet and parked.

"Yes, but not in over ten years. It's too pricey for client dinners or girls' night out."

"I thought maybe a date might have taken you."

"Nope. You're the first."

"*Finally*, I'm first at something with you." He grinned and pumped his fist just as a valet opened my door and offered me a hand getting out, which I needed in this skirt. Quinn had practically had to boost me in.

Inside the opulent main hall, Quinn took my coat and checked it along with his, and we admired the fireplace, stained glass windows, and immense staircase before asking for our table. "Imagine playing on that staircase," Quinn whispered to me as we were shown into a dimly lit circular room with high ceilings and ornate wood paneling. "Or anywhere in this house."

I giggled and whispered back, "Naked hide and seek."

He groaned. "Don't tempt me."

We were shown to a beautifully set table for two along the perimeter of the room, and Quinn waited for the host to seat me before lowering himself into his chair. (Later, when I excused myself to use the bathroom, he stood when I got up and when I returned as well. I'm the least romantic person I know, but I do find that kind of old-fashioned courtesy attractive—especially when I know the dirty mind behind the courtly manners. It was like another little game, a secret we shared.)

We dined on calamari, beef Wellington, and grilled vegetables, polishing off a bottle of Barolo in between delectable bites. When the dessert plates had been cleared—we'd devoured something called Chocolate Cartier, which included strawberries covered in chocolate, my favorite way to eat fruit—Quinn reached into his suit jacket and pulled out a small white box.

Since it was flat and square, I felt no rising panic that I'd somehow led him to believe a ring was a good idea. Instead, I smiled at him.

"What's this?"

"A present." He set it on the table.

"This meal was my present. And I loved every minute of it."

He nudged the box toward me. "Open it."

Giving him a suspicious look, I slid the box closer and took off the top. "Oh my God!" I gasped, putting my hands to my cheeks, which felt hot beneath my fingers. "Quinn, it's beautiful. I love it."

It was a silver circle pendant, about one inch in diameter, attached in two spots to a delicate silver chain so it would lie flat on my collarbone.

"I'm glad. It's nothing fancy, but I saw it this week and thought of you. I noticed you don't wear a lot of jewelry."

"I don't at all. This is perfect—a little sparkle, a little elegance. I love it, really." My throat felt tight, and I swallowed hard.

"It came with that little card that tells about the symbolism of it."

I picked up the card the necklace was resting on and read aloud. "Karma. What goes around comes around… Wear your necklace as a reminder to keep the circle positive, peaceful, and loving." I met his eyes.

"I thought it was a nice message. Hope you don't think it's too sappy."

"Not at all. I think it's a beautiful message. Should I put it on?"

He looked pleased. "If you want to."

Carefully undoing the clasp, I lowered my head, placed the necklace around my neck and fastened it. When I looked up, he was taking a picture.

I laughed. "Really? Right now, during this nice, private moment?"

"Not sorry. You look happy and beautiful."

"I feel happy and beautiful," I said honestly, touching the circle with my fingertips. My entire body hummed with warmth. It almost felt like being a little drunk, but I knew it wasn't the wine. "And I'll wear this often, Quinn."

"Good. It looks perfect on you." His eyes dropped to his coffee cup as he toyed with the handle. "And I think it's true, the idea that you get back what you put out there. Since my mom died, I've thought a lot about what I'm, you know, putting out there. And what I want back."

"Yeah?" I rested my chin on my hands, elbows on the table.

"She put such pure, selfless love out there. Worked so hard and always took pride in what she did, whether it was cleaning someone's house, cooking at the restaurant, or raising a son on her own."

"She was very proud of you. Nothing made her happier than talking about you." I sighed, thinking of my own mother. "I have no idea what makes my mother happy beyond her work. What she wants to put out there or get back. I don't think it's love."

Quinn looked up at me. "No?"

"Actually, I don't know. That's terrible, isn't it? That I don't know my mother well enough to know what makes her happy?"

"Some people are hard to know."

"Yeah, but she's my *mother*." I sat back, dropping my hands in my lap. "And other than her job, I have no clue what makes her excited to get up in the morning. What's she passionate about?"

"Maybe it's the research she does. That helps a lot of people."

"I guess. That's just so *in her head*, you know? It doesn't connect her to anyone. She seems so…closed off sometimes. Just sharing a roof with my father and living in her own little world by herself. They don't even share a bedroom."

Quinn looked at me for a moment. "Are you worried that she's *un*happy?"

"Maybe." I thought for a second, words on the tip of my tongue. "Or maybe I'm worried about turning out like her."

"In what way?"

"I don't know. Forget I said anything." Suddenly self-conscious, I fussed with the knot of hair at my neck.

"No, come on." Quinn leaned forward on his elbows. "Talk to me."

God, he was so handsome. And he was *good* to me—I wasn't an easy person to get close to, and he tolerated all my quirks, made me feel beautiful and sexy, respected my boundaries even after a month had gone by. He deserved more of me, and he was asking for it.

I bit my lip. "Do you think I'm too closed off? Too unaffectionate? That I might end up alone and unhappy because I won't let anybody in?"

He didn't answer right away. "I think," he said slowly, "you're a very loyal person who shows love in her own way, on her own terms."

"But what about the way I don't like all the mushy romantic stuff or talking about feelings or being touched all the time? Am I cold-blooded? Just weird? Am I too in my head? Why don't I believe in love like other people do? Why do I feel like it's me who knows the truth and everyone else is deluded, yet everyone else is destined to be much happier than I'll ever be?" By the time I stopped talking, I was a little tearful, and Quinn reached for my hand. I let him have it.

"First, I *know* you're warm-blooded. In fact, I'd venture to say your blood runs downright scalding sometimes. And I love that about you—you might keep your cool all day long, but then it comes out of nowhere, this intense heat." He squeezed my hand.

"I can't get enough of it, and I'm not saying that to make you feel bad—I mean it as a compliment. When something is in short supply, there's always high demand."

I couldn't resist. "Is that a short joke?"

"No. It isn't." He squeezed my hand again. "And you're not weird. Plenty of people don't like sappy stuff or want to be in constant physical contact. Everyone has a different comfort level with physical affection. Yours and mine might be different, but that doesn't mean yours is wrong. Do I think you're too in your head sometimes? Yes. Do I think that means you'll wind up alone and unhappy? No."

"Thanks. I think."

He smiled. "As for love, I don't know why you don't believe. Maybe you won't let yourself."

"What?" My skin prickled with gooseflesh.

"Maybe you're so good at being in your head that your rational mind has entirely overruled your emotions, and that suits you just fine."

His words jogged my memory. "Margot said something like that to me about a month ago, when I was complaining about how you wanted to date me."

He looked amused. "Oh?"

"Yeah, she said I don't let myself enjoy sex with men I date because I don't want to have a reason to give them a real chance. And that I use great sex as a reason to avoid dating them at all."

"Like you tried to do with me," he said, his eyebrows rising. "Very astute. She knows you."

I frowned. "She does. But what does all this mean? Have I just been lying to myself all this time? Sabotaging my own chance to be happy with someone?"

"Hey." He took my fingers and wiggled them. "No frowning. The point of the gift was not to give you an existential crisis. It was to give you a pretty little thing to remind you that what you give is what you get, and what I want to give you right now is an orgasm."

Yes. That was enough to turn my worry into a different kind of tension—one I knew how to deal with, one that could be easily and joyously relieved, one that made me ache to get my hands on him. "Chances are good you'll *get* one, too."

"Just one?"

I lifted my shoulders playfully. "We'll see what happens."

We paid the bill and picked up our coats, and after he slipped mine onto my shoulders, he spoke low in my ear. "Your ass in that red skirt has me so hard right now."

Giggling, I pulled on my gloves and spoke softly over my shoulder. "Patience, Mr. Wolf. Give a girl a little time to frolic in the woods before you grab her ass." I turned to face him and rose on tiptoe to whisper in his ear. "Want to come home and frolic with me?"

He grabbed my wrist and yanked me toward the door without another word.

CHAPTER
TWENTY

Jaime

He loomed over me in the dark as I shivered on the kitchen floor.

"Nowhere to run, little girl," he said, his tone dark but delighted. "I've chased you all through the woods. I've chased you out of your pretty clothes. I've chased you right onto your knees." He was naked and hard, and now he took his dick in his hand, stroking it while I watched, open-mouthed and wide-eyed. "Now what am I going to do with you?"

On my hands and knees, I sat back on my heels. "What do you want to do with me?"

"Eat you, of course. Tear you apart." He worked his hand slowly up and down his cock, and I felt my nipples tingling. "But I'm a patient wolf, and I'm not completely without a sense of decorum. Any last requests?"

I licked my lips. "Yes. One."

"Which is?"

"I want to watch you."

"Watch me?" Surprise colored his words, but I thought it might be pretend, since he kept his fist tight around his shaft and jerked hard a couple times. "What do you mean, little girl?"

Fuck, he was hot. My eyes had adjusted to the dark enough to appreciate the gorgeous lines of his body in the dark, the swell of the muscles, the motion of his arm. I'd given him a hand job before, but I'd never watched him (or any other guy) do it to himself, and suddenly it seemed like the hottest thing ever. I'd felt his orgasm inside me, heard the gasp and groan of it, tasted it on my tongue—now I wanted to *see* it. "I want to watch you do that."

His hand slowed again. "You know I like you to be specific. Tell me exactly what you want or you won't get it."

Quinn never let me get away with skirting around my dirtiest desires. *If you think it, you should say it*, he said. *Believe me, I want to hear it.*

"I want to see your hands on your body. I want to watch you lose control. I want to watch you make yourself come while you look at me."

His chest hitched with rapid breaths. "You're such a naughty little girl."

He didn't know the half of it—there were all kinds of things running through my mind right now.

"I am," I said, getting to my knees, running my hands up my thighs. "Because I've thought about it before."

"Yeah?" His eyes were glued to my hands, which roamed over my breasts, down my stomach, between my legs. He moved his thumb over the shiny tip of his cock, and my clit throbbed.

"Yes. When you first moved in, I'd imagine you in bed below me getting yourself off while I did the same in my bed." I slipped one fingertip inside myself and rubbed the wetness over my clit.

"I probably was. Fuck." His hand moved faster over his cock, which was thick with veins and darker than the skin on his thighs.

"Did you think about me?"

"Yes," he rasped. "Fuck yes, I did." His ab muscles flexed as he jerked his fist up and down in quick, tight motions. "Are you wet?"

"Drenched." Filled to bursting with the desire to please him, to do things with him I'd never done with anyone else, I pushed my finger in deeper. "Want to feel?"

His eyes nearly came out of his head. Before he could answer, I moved a little closer and put my wet fingertip between his legs, brushing over a sensitive spot, then sliding it back a little to test him. Would he let me? I wasn't sure how far I should go—this was something I'd thought about but never done before. I'd never felt close enough to anyone to try it. But I wanted to with Quinn, wanted to see what it would do to him, wanted to experience that sense of power inherent in penetrating someone, getting inside him. What was that like?

"Yes," he hissed through clenched teeth. "Oh my fucking God, yes."

Slowly and carefully, I pushed in deeper, delighted by the way it made him moan and curse, shocked at the tight, hot grip around my finger. With my other hand, I rubbed my clit, bringing both of us that much closer.

"Fuck. I'm gonna come," he growled, barely able to speak. "So hard…"

"Right here," I whispered, moving my other hand to my breasts.

With a strangled moan, he angled his dick toward my chest. His fist tightened and slowed, and I watched as he came on my tits in quick, hot bursts, his ass clenching my fingertip. I couldn't move, couldn't talk, couldn't take my eyes off him. It was the hottest thing I'd ever seen.

When it was over, I fell back onto my hands and sat on the floor, panting as hard as if the orgasm had been mine.

He dropped to his knees, pushed my legs apart and lowered his head between my thighs. Propping myself on my elbows, I watched him devour me like I was covered in Chocolate Cartier.

He dipped his tongue inside, licking upward in short, tantalizing strokes. "So sweet," he murmured. "How can such a wicked little girl taste so sweet?"

I'd been close to orgasm before, and as he swirled his tongue over my clit, I found myself right back at the edge, my lower body humming with pleasure, my breath coming fast, my knees opening wider.

He slid a hand up my stomach to my chest, which was dripping with his cum. Stretching his fingers, he smeared it all over my breasts while sucking my clit into his mouth. The sight of it sent me barreling over the edge, the orgasm tearing me to pieces like he said he would. I cried out repeatedly as all the tension inside me eased in blissful beats against his tongue.

"Enough, enough," I panted when the sensitivity grew too much to bear. "Stop."

He got to his knees and looked down at me. Without a word, he took the hand from my chest and rubbed two fingers over my lips. I opened my mouth and licked them, sucked the salty sweetness off the tips, eyes locked on his.

The moment was so intense, it frightened me. In the silence I heard myself speaking words I didn't want to say, feeling things I didn't want to feel. I was on the hard kitchen floor, but it didn't feel solid beneath me. It was splintering, breaking apart piece by piece—I had to get up soon or I'd fall through it.

"Wow," I forced myself to say. "I'm a mess."

Quinn made a noise between a groan and a laugh. "It's so fucking hot. Do we have to clean you up?"

"Yes, we do." I sat up all the way and looked down at my chest. "Or, rather, I do."

"Let me do it." Quinn popped to his feet, turned on the faucet, and started opening drawers. "Where are your towels?"

"They're in the third drawer down, but I think I might just get in the shower and rinse off."

"Oh. OK." He turned off the water and gave me a hand getting to my feet. "Sorry. I guess I did make a bit of a mess."

"Hey." I didn't want him to feel bad. "I asked for the mess, and I loved every second of it. It was my idea."

"You did ask for it. That surprised me."

"Really? After all the stuff we've done?"

"Well, yeah. That's like a personal thing, jerking off. Not usually done in the company of others. In fact, never, for me."

"No?"

He shrugged. "No. If there was a girl around, why would I? And no girl ever asked."

"*Finally*, I'm first at something with you." I pumped a fist in the air as I repeated his words from earlier tonight.

He laughed. "And what about you? Ever asked anyone to do that to you before?"

"Nope. Never even thought about it."

"Yes! Another first. I feel like a god."

I giggled. "I can give you a third one if you want."

"Anal?" he asked hopefully.

"Uh, we'll talk. But no, I was actually thinking of inviting you into the shower with me." A shower was OK, right? It was personal but not *too* too personal. It wasn't like doing it without a condom or sleeping over or peeing while he was in the bathroom.

"You're inviting me into your shower?" He put a hand on his chest. "My God! This means you believe in love now, doesn't it! I finally did it! And all I had to do was fuck my hand and shoot my load on your chest. How did I not think of it sooner?"

I shook my head and started walking away. "You're insane. And I don't like insane people in my shower, so I'm taking back my invite."

"No way." He followed me through my bedroom and into the bath. "You're stuck with me, sweet pea. Face it."

After turning on the light and blinking at the sudden brightness, I opened the sliding shower door and turned on the water. "Stuck with you, huh?" Facing him again, I pretended to look him over from head to toe. God, I was so lucky. Tonight was *perfect*. "I suppose there are worse things."

CHAPTER TWENTY-ONE

Quinn

I might not have a lot of talents, but I can get hard again pretty quickly after an orgasm. It's not something you can pay the bills with (unless you're Logan O'Toole, but that's a different story), and it really only comes in handy in very specific circumstances, but I'm kind of proud of it.

That said, I didn't want to fuck Jaime in the shower.

OK, that's a lie—I *wanted* to, but I told myself I wouldn't.

I had a good reason.

Jaime could make anything about sex. This wasn't only because she was the sexiest woman I'd ever known without even trying, but because she felt comfortable with sex. It was safe ground for her.

I wanted new ground.

It had been a month since we'd been dating, and I was crazy about her. I couldn't *say* that to her of course, because it would probably make her rock back and forth in agony, but the more time I spent with her, both in and out of bed, the more convinced I was that she and I had something special. I'd never had as much fun with anyone—she made me laugh at myself and let me laugh at her. I got such a kick out of listening to her tell me all the random stuff she knew—she was so curious about the stories behind things and people. Maybe it's what made her go into advertising.

"Did you know Faygo red pop was created by Russian bakers who used their frosting recipe to create a new drink?"

"Did you know the Disney princesses don't look at each other when they're grouped together to preserve their individual mythologies?"

"Did you know that in New York, they call Coney Islands Michigan hot dogs?"

She listened when I needed to talk, too. I felt like she understood me.

And I understood her—I couldn't rush her.

She hadn't said as much (surprise, surprise), but I had the feeling she felt more for me than she usually felt for men she dated or men she just slept with. What she'd said tonight sort of confirmed it—in the past, she hadn't allowed great sex to inspire feelings, and she'd never allowed herself to develop feelings where there was great sex. We had both, but where she was comfortable expressing her sexuality, she was totally *un*comfortable expressing her feelings, so she used one to do the other.

I wanted to encourage her to let her feelings show in ways that didn't involve an orgasm. I didn't need words necessarily, but this was nice—she was letting me into her personal space after sex, inviting me to stay a little longer with her. I wanted to show her that I liked it, not because it would lead to more sex, but because it made me feel closer to her. I wanted her to like feeling closer to me, and more importantly, to be OK with it.

So I washed her hair (I'd, um, sullied it a bit), soaped her body, and rinsed her off while ignoring my dick, which was not in favor of the no-shower-sex plan. In fact, he was *firmly* against it and showed his displeasure by twitching agitatedly every few minutes. Once, it hit Jaime on the butt, and I apologized.

She giggled. "Don't be sorry. It's funny, I like it."

"Funny? My dick is funny to you?" Yes, jokes were good. Jokes would distract me.

"I'm sorry, let me try again." She peeked at it. "You're right. It's a very serious cock. Very no-nonsense. Businesslike. Maybe even presidential."

I pinched her ass. "I thought you were going to say stiff."

She glanced down again. "Not yet, but getting there."

"Don't look. You'll only encourage it, and I'm trying not to get hard."

"Why on earth would you do that?"

"Because I'm trying to be a good guy and show you that we can have fun together without having sex."

"Silly boy," she whispered, stroking me softly. "I know we can have fun together without having sex. But I happen to love having sex with you."

My plan to not fuck her was unraveling at an alarming speed—the speed with which my dick was getting hard. I made one last effort. "I know, and I love it too, but I also like just being close to you. Talking to you. Listening to you." *But please put your finger in my ass again. That was fucking amazing.*

"Listen to me," she said, sliding her hand up and down my flesh. "I feel closer to you than I've ever felt to any man, ever. I've let you in deeper. Revealed more of myself. And my favorite way to share that with you, the only way I'm good at, is with my body. It's the language I speak. Does that make sense?"

Her words stirred something inside me, and it was enough to overcome my restraint. "Yes," I said, letting my hands go where they wanted, putting my lips on her warm, wet skin. "Yes."

She laughed throatily, slinging an arm around my neck. "You're so fucking easy."

CHAPTER TWENTY-TWO

Jamie

So fucking easy.
It would be so fucking easy to just let him slide inside me, hot and hard and wet.

We'd made it onto my bed, ostensibly to get a condom, but neither of us had reached for one. Too impatient to even dry off, our bodies dripped onto my sheets as we lay on our sides and clung to each other, my leg thrown over his hip, his cock trapped between us, our lips locked in a feverish kiss.

But should we?

The one time we'd done it without a condom I'd been able to dismiss as a spontaneous, heat-of-the-moment oopsy, like a crime of passion. I wouldn't be able to do the same this time if I kept thinking about it—this would clearly be premeditated.

But I wanted it. I wanted it so badly.

I wanted him to have me in a way no one else ever had. I wanted to share myself in a way I never had. I wanted us to experience each other skin to skin, nothing between us. This whole night had been a series of breaking down barriers, from our conversation at dinner to the sexual adventure in the kitchen to inviting him into my shower—and the more I opened myself to him, the further I wanted him to go.

I'd told him things tonight I'd never told anyone, done things to him and let him do things to me I'd been scared to even think about before. And he hadn't judged me—he never judged me. He was so patient with me, so sweet, so stubborn, so sure that I had the capacity to love someone.

How could I tell him what that meant to me? I wasn't good at revealing myself with words, but I could show him.

And I would.

"Quinn," I whispered frantically. "I want you inside me. Fuck the condom."

"Are you sure?" His eyes searched mine in the dark.

"Yes." My entire body ached for him to fill it. "I want you so badly right now, I can't describe it—I want you so badly it hurts."

"I want you too." He took over, taking his cock in his hand and guiding it between my legs.

I was so wet he slid in easily, but he went slow, his eyes closing. When he was buried inside me, he opened them, and we held still for a moment, just looking at each other.

My heart was thundering in my chest, and I felt his doing the same. His hand slid over my hip, pulling me tighter to his body, and I hitched my leg up even higher, making the angle even better.

"This feels so good," he whispered. "I don't even want to move, it will be over too quickly. But I have to…" He began to move his lower body in that slow, sinuous motion I loved, the one that had him rubbing all the right places, inside and out. "You make me so hard."

"Don't worry, I'm with you," I said, matching his rhythm with my hips. "I promise."

It didn't take long for the intensity to build, especially knowing we were doing it without a condom—breaking a rule!—*on purpose*. Before long, Quinn had me on my back, his cock driving hard and deep, my nails digging into his ass, our bodies damp with water and sweat. Higher and higher we climbed, desperate for release, unable to stop, but unwilling to leave the other behind.

"Now," he said hotly, his breath in my ear. "Come for me. Let me feel you come on my cock before I—"

I lost the rest of what he was saying, my senses abandoned, my universe reduced to the shared pulse between us. I don't know where my orgasm stopped or his began; they ran together, fed off each other, kept us clutching at one another, trying against all odds to get deeper, get closer, get *more*.

When his body collapsed on top of mine, I felt grateful for the weight of it, the way it grounded me, stopped me from floating into the sky. I held him to me with my arms and legs, pressed my lips to his neck, breathed him in deep.

"Are you OK?" He lifted his chest off me and looked down. "Sorry, I didn't mean to crush you."

"You're not. Come back." I pulled on his shoulders. "I wasn't suffocating, I was sniffing you."

He laughed and lowered himself a little, propping himself on his elbows above my shoulders. "Is this OK?"

"Yes." I ran my hands up his sides, over his chest, and into his hair. "Just don't leave yet."

"OK."

I looked up at him and realized it wasn't that I didn't want him to leave yet; I didn't want him to leave *at all*.

I wanted him next to me all night. I wanted to fall asleep in his arms and wake up with him beside me. I wanted to talk more about his mom and my mom and our childhoods. I wanted to whisper about the future and what it might hold. I wanted to laugh about my rules and how he'd somehow convinced me to break every one of them without even appearing to try. I wanted to let him all the way in.

I wanted to love him.

"Quinn," I whispered, brushing the hair back from his face. "I don't want you to leave me tonight."

He hesitated. "Does that mean you want me to stay?"

"Yes."

"The night?"

"Yes." *Please don't tease me right now. Don't ask me what it means. Don't remind me of the rules. Just trust me. Let me give you more, a little at a time.*

"OK," he said, kissing me softly. "I'll stay."

I drifted off to sleep spooned in Quinn's embrace.

"You're sure you're OK?" he asked for the tenth time. "I'm not crowding you?"

"For fuck's sake, Quinn."

"Well, I'm sorry, but I know how you get."

"What I'm getting right now is irritated. I'm tired, go to sleep."

"OK, OK."

I'd like to say we spooned all night, but I probably only lasted about twenty minutes before I got too hot, rolled onto my stomach, and hitched up my knee between us.

But I tried—that counts, right?

And even though we weren't wrapped up in each other all night, I did like knowing he was there in my bed. The couple times I woke up and remembered the night before, I smiled into my pillow, happier than I'd been in a long time.

In the morning, I woke up first and lay on my side, facing him. He was beautiful even in his sleep, his features completely relaxed. Lying on his back, he had one arm thrown over his head, and I had the weirdest urge to sniff his armpit.

Don't judge. As armpits go, it's pretty much perfect.

I refrained from pit sniffing, but I couldn't resist touching his chest, which was visible above the top of the sheet. Scooting a little closer, I traced a line down the center of his sternum with my fingertips, then covered one pectoral muscle with my palm.

His eyes opened, and he smiled. "Hey."

I smiled too. "Hey."

"How'd you sleep?"

"Great. You?"

"Same. What time is it?"

"I have no idea. I never brought my phone in here."

"Me either. I'm not even sure where my clothes are. That seems to happen a lot around you."

I giggled. "I think they're in a variety of places between our two flats."

"It was a good night."

"It was." I kept looking at him, waiting for the remorse to kick in, the urge for him to leave, the compulsion to be by myself…but I felt none of that. Not only was I happy he was there, but I didn't want him to go.

"We broke a rule," he said, a sly grin on his face. "Are you mad at us?"

I propped my head in my hand. "Actually, no. Can you believe it?"

"No." His eyes went wide, twinkling with mischief. "Does this mean…"

I reached out and put two fingers over his lips. "No. It means I had fun and I'm glad you stayed the night."

He kissed my fingers and grabbed my wrist. "Party pooper. Get over here." Pulling me close, he gathered me into his chest, arms wrapped around my head, chin resting on top of it. "Give me ten seconds of excessive cuddling, and then I'll let you go."

I groaned for effect, but if he could have seen my face, he'd have known how happy I was.

What on earth was happening?

Three days later, I met Claire and Margot for our weekly GNO. It was my turn to pick the place, and I chose Standby, a relatively new bar in the Belt Alley that had great cocktails and delicious small plates.

I got there first, ordered a Vermilion Fizz, and took a minute to text Quinn.

Hey. At Standby with girls. See you tonight?

Definitely. Have fun and knock when you get home.

After that there was a little bumblebee emoji, which Quinn had designated the "love bug." Shaking my head, I quickly checked his Instagram account, where he'd posted a pic from this morning. I'd probably looked at it a hundred times already today, but I couldn't resist peeking at it again. We'd still been lying in his bed, and he'd snapped a selfie right as he kissed my cheek, which I didn't even realize because I was laughing at something he'd said and my eyes were closed. My hair was a mess and the picture was kind of blurry, but it captured *us* perfectly. His caption was simply *This girl.* #wcw #sweetpea

"What are you smiling about?" Claire took off her coat and hung it on the chair across the table from me.

"Nothing." I tucked my phone into my purse, embarrassed to be caught grinning like an idiot at a screen.

"Does nothing stand about six foot two, have piercing blue eyes, and a great big dick?"

I shrugged, but I couldn't keep the blush from my cheeks. "Maybe."

"God, what is going *on* with you?" she demanded, sliding onto the seat. "If I didn't know better, I'd say you were in love."

I coughed in protest, even as the room started to spin. "Please. I'm not in love. I'm just…enjoying myself. Isn't that allowed?"

"Of course it's *allowed*. It's just very *unlike* you to enjoy yourself with one guy for this long."

"I know. It does feel a bit strange," I admitted as Margot breezed in and sat down next to Claire.

"What does?" she asked, shrugging out of her jacket and glancing around. "Do they have a coat check here? Or a rack?"

"I don't know. Here, I'll take it." I reached out and took her heavy camel coat and set it on the bench next to me.

"Thanks. Now what's strange?" she asked.

"Being in love," Claire interjected.

"Being with Quinn," I said firmly, giving Claire the evil eye.

The server came over with my drink and took their orders. When he was gone, Margot asked, "But is it good strange? Being in a couple?"

"Yeah." I took a sip. "Mm, that's good." Everything tasted good these last few days.

"Did you break the sleepover rule?" Claire's expression was smug, and I knew the color was back in my cheeks again.

"Uh, we did, actually. On Saturday night." I took another sip. "And then again on Sunday, Monday, and Tuesday."

Their jaws dropped, and then they looked at each other.

I burst out laughing. "You guys look so funny."

"I can't believe it," Claire said, shaking her head. "You've spent four nights in a row together?"

"Yes. I can hardly believe it either." We'd spent the first two in my flat and the last two in his. Who knew where we'd end up tonight?

"And you're OK with it?" Margot scrutinized my face. "You don't feel smothered?"

"No. It's kind of insane." I played with the stem of my glass as I confessed. "I'm actually liking the closeness. I mean, I don't like him right on top of me all the time, I still like my personal space, but…" I shrugged. "I like when he's there."

"Holy shit. You've got a boyfriend, Jaime." Margot looked amused.

"What? No, I don't." I felt my face getting hotter, and I focused on taking a drink of my cold cocktail.

"You do. You so do." Grinning, she sat back as the server set their drinks down. "It's nothing to be ashamed of. You don't need a support group."

"I know. I just…don't really want a boyfriend," I insisted. "We agreed not to put that kind of label on things, and I think it's helping me be comfortable with what we're doing."

"Which is what?"

"Dating. Having fun. Enjoying each other's company." I paused. "Often naked."

Claire rolled her eyes. "Sounds like a boyfriend

to me."

"Claire, please. A boyfriend is more serious. Like Tripp. Tripp's a boyfriend."

"For now, anyway." Margot sighed.

"Did you talk to him yet?" I asked, kind of hoping to get off the subject of Quinn. The truth was, I didn't know exactly what we were doing or what to call it or what would happen next week when he moved out. I was hoping we'd be able to keep it just like this—light and fun, strings but no labels, meaningful but not serious. Anything more than that, and I started to hyperventilate.

"No. I didn't want to ruin Valentine's Day. We were having dinner with Mimi and Deuce," she said glumly. "But I can't put it off much longer. I'm miserable not knowing."

Because that is what serious relationships do to people, I reminded myself. *That's what falling in love does—jacks up their hopes and creates impossible expectations. Misery is inevitable.*

But later, as Quinn moved inside me and the stars exploded and the heavens opened up and the earth spun so wildly out of control I clung to him like a terrified child, I knew I had to be careful.

All my rules were broken.
All my walls were down.

∬

I slept alone that night.

CHAPTER TWENTY-THREE

Quinn

My condo was ready. I hadn't said anything to Jaime over Valentine's weekend, and then it had been so intense the following weeks, sleeping together every night, that I hadn't even *thought* about moving out. I told myself that I was paid up through the end of February and could take my time moving to the new place, but when a week went by and I still hadn't even called the movers, I admitted to myself what was happening.

I was in love with her, and I was scared to break the spell.

It was like something magical had happened on Valentine's Day, and I'm not just talking about her finger in my ass.

I mean like *real* magic.

Suddenly she was opening up to me about her feelings, inviting me to stay the night, letting me hold her closer, tighter, longer. Without words, she was telling me that I made her happy, that she trusted me, that she cared for me. Sometimes I even felt like she was on the verge of telling me she loved me—and I knew I'd almost said it to her a bunch of times. But neither of us ever went through with it.

Just another game of chicken.

But all day, every day, all I thought about was her—wondering what she was doing, remembering things from the night before, anticipating when I'd see her next, thinking of things I wanted to do with her, show to her, say to her. It was almost ridiculous—I felt like a twelve year old with his first crush. I couldn't get enough of her.

Occasionally I felt her pull back slightly, nights where she left my bed and went to sleep in her own, times when she slipped out of my arms when I would've kept holding her, but I understood her need to keep some personal space, maintain some distance. It made her feel safe, in control of her feelings. And those instances were the exception, not the rule.

She wanted to be with me more often now, even if it was just sitting next to me on the couch while she worked. When an unusually warm day caused a big snowmelt, she wanted to take a walk and even held my hand part of the time. She listened to me blather on about what courses to take next term, debate whether I'd make a good teacher (she thought I would make a great one), and fret about what the smartest investments would be for my savings if I went in that direction, since it meant I'd never make the kind of money I'd made modeling.

"Who cares?" she'd said. "You should do what you're passionate about, not what makes the most money."

I knew she was right, but I was also trying to think ahead, and Jaime was a woman who focused on the present. I had to think about the reality of living, and hopefully supporting a family, on a teacher's salary, unless I kept a hand in modeling part-time, which would mean less free time and more traveling. I had to give it some thought.

And like it or not, I had to move out of Jaime's house.

Yesterday, I'd called the movers and arranged for them to get my furniture out of storage and deliver it to my new place on Tuesday, which was two days away. I was hoping nothing would change, that we'd be able to make time to see each other almost as often as we did now. It would take more effort, since we'd be separated by more than just a staircase, but my new building wasn't really that far from where she worked. I'd also been thinking about a little vacation. It had been such a cold winter—maybe she'd like to go sit on a beach somewhere. She'd once told me that was her kind of getaway.

I'll talk to her about it tonight, I thought as I made dinner for us. If she seemed upset about my leaving, maybe the idea of a little sand and sun together would soften the blow.

My phone vibrated on the kitchen counter, and I saw her name on the screen. "Hello?"

"Hey, it's me."

"Hi. How's it going?" I stirred the pot of tomato sauce I had on the stove.

"It's kinda bad here," she said quietly, as if she didn't want anyone to hear. It was Sunday night and we'd been planning on dinner in and watching Netflix, but about an hour earlier, she'd gotten a call from one of her friends that there was some sort of emergency, and she should go to Margot's house right away.

"What happened? Is everyone OK?"

"Everyone's fine physically, but Margot and her boyfriend broke up, and she's a mess."

"Oh. Sorry to hear that." I set the spoon on a paper towel and turned the heat off under the pasta water. If she was going to be late, I didn't want to cook the noodles yet. "Think you'll be a while?"

She sighed. "Probably. I totally understand if you want to eat without me."

"I don't mind waiting. Want to call me when you're on your way?"

"OK. I will."

She didn't sound like herself, but maybe she was just worried about her friend. "Everything OK with you?"

"Yeah, I'm fine. Just sad for her. And I'm never sure what to say at these times."

After we hung up, I occupied myself throwing clothing and linens into boxes for the move. I felt like a selfish asshole even thinking it, but I hoped Margot's breakup wasn't going to fuck with Jaime's head.

We were in a good place right now, but we'd only just gotten here.

CHAPTER TWENTY-FOUR

Jaime

I'd never seen Margot like this. Not once in the thirteen years I'd known her. She'd always had a boyfriend—we joked that she was a serial monogamist—but her relationships had always ended amicably or she'd been the one to break things off.

This was something else entirely.

Calm, cool, cultured Margot Thurber Lewiston was having a very unbecoming ugly cry on her bedroom floor. Curled in a ball with a (probably heirloom) quilt pulled tightly around her shoulders, she sobbed and howled, her beautiful face contorted in misery and covered with tears and snot.

"Margot, come on. It's going to be OK." On her knees at Margot's side, Claire patted her back. "Want me to get you a hanky?"

"Want a pillow?" I offered from where I sat on Margot's bed. The expensive sheets were all untucked and twisted as if she'd thrown a violent tantrum on her bed and then rolled right off it onto the hardwood floor. She had a rug beneath her, but still—she couldn't have been very comfortable.

Not that she cared about comfort. She didn't answer either one of us, just kept crying and crying, her slender body shuddering pitifully beneath the quilt. She was nearly hoarse from wailing, but nothing we said had consoled her so far.

My own throat was tight—I'd never felt so helpless. Truth be told, I wasn't good at this. I didn't know what to say because I'd never been in her position. Even my shittiest breakups in college, before I'd sworn off relationships, hadn't done this to me. I hadn't cried like this since—

Quinn.

It suddenly struck me that the way Margot was carrying on reminded me of the way I'd cried the night I'd told Quinn I loved him and he'd laughed at me.

Turning off the warning bell in my head, I got down on the floor with a little square pillow embroidered with the words Like Mother, Like Daughter. I looked at it for a second before putting it down near Margot's face.

"Here, Gogo. Put your head on this. You're going to have a terrible headache as it is."

Nothing. More choked sobs.

"Margot, honey, talk to us." Claire tried to lean down and make eye contact, but Margot's puffy eyes were shut tight. We still didn't know exactly what happened. After getting her text asking us to please come to her house as soon as we could, we'd rushed over and found her like this. She'd nodded yes when we asked if something had happened with Tripp, but we had no other details.

Exchanging a worried glance with Claire, I stroked Margot's hair. Usually blown out to smooth, shiny perfection, right now it looked and felt like it might contain a couple bird nests. Maybe a squirrel corpse or two.

"OK then, cry it out," I said, realizing that there was no stopping this train. "We'll be right here when you're ready to talk." I lay down on the floor too, curling up on my side, hands tucked under my cheek.

"Yep." Claire lay down on the other side of her and patted her shoulder. "We're not going anywhere."

A few minutes ticked by, and Margot's sobs slowed, then quieted. Finally, she took a long, shaky breath. "OK." She exhaled. "OK. I think I need some whiskey."

"You got it," I said, hopping to my feet. I might not be good at soothing a broken heart, but shooting whiskey? *That* I could do.

I hurried down the steps of Margot's beautiful townhouse and pulled a bottle of Two James Grass Widow Bourbon from a kitchen cupboard. Tucking it under my arm, I grabbed three little glasses from another shelf and headed back up.

When I reached her bedroom, Margot was sitting up against the bed, blowing her nose in a tissue. Claire sat next to her, holding the box.

"Just what the doctor ordered," I said, setting the glasses down and sitting cross-legged, facing them. I opened the bottle and poured about an inch into each glass, handing one to Margot and one to Claire. Setting the bottle aside, I picked up mine and we all took a sip.

Margot sighed. "God, I need this." She tipped her glass back again, finishing the contents.

"Easy, hon," Claire warned.

I picked up the bottle and poured her some more. "So easy."

It almost made her smile. "Fuck, you guys. My head."

"I can imagine," I said. Her eyes were so red and puffy, I didn't know how she could see. "Want to tell us what happened?"

She sipped again before talking. "Probably exactly what you think. I brought up getting engaged last night at dinner, and he changed the subject. I tried again when we got back here, and he went home with a headache. I tried a third time this morning after brunch, and he finally admitted he'd been putting off telling me something for a while because he didn't want to hurt me."

"What did he say?" Claire asked.

"That he changed his mind. He doesn't want to get married."

"Doesn't want to get married *now*? Or ever?" I wondered.

Margot nodded. "That's what I asked. And he said definitely not now, and maybe not ever."

"Well, what the fuck?" I frowned. "Why did he lead you to believe otherwise for the last three years?"

"I asked him that too. He said people change."

"Within a few months?" Claire snapped. "He just asked you about a ring in December!"

"I know," Margot said before a big swallow of bourbon, "but now he says he's perfectly happy with the way things are and he doesn't want anything to change."

Happiness is always a for-now thing, I heard myself telling Quinn the night I laid out the rules for him.

But don't you think it's possible to know that something or someone would always make you happy? he'd asked.

Lately the question had begun to haunt me.

"That's bullshit." Claire sat up taller. "So he just wants you to wait around until he decides *he's* ready for things to change?"

"Basically." Margot shrugged, her eyes filling. "But there's no guarantee he'll ever want things to change. He refused to make any promises."

So what? I thought. *Promises, like rules, could be broken.* But I said nothing.

"God, I want to punch his smug chin right now," Claire said. "I'm sorry, but I hate his chin. The way he points it at people."

"It's OK, I hate it right now too." Margot drank a little more. "And the sex lately has been bad, you guys."

"Really?" I blinked at her.

She nodded. "I don't know why, exactly. It seemed perfectly fine for three years and then it just got—I don't know. Routine. Too fast."

"But doesn't that always happen over time?" I asked. "I mean, you can't expect that initial spark to last for years, can you?" Although, to be honest, I couldn't imagine the spark between Quinn and me dying out. What the hell?

"Sure, you can," Claire argued. "I've seen plenty of couples who have great sexual chemistry and have been together for years. Look at my parents! It's embarrassing how much they touch each other all the time!"

"And it's not like I expect fireworks every time," Margot said. "I'd settle for an orgasm once a month, even."

I gaped at her. "Once a *month*? Remind me why you want to marry this guy."

"Because we're right for each other! And I don't understand what went wrong," she said, setting her glass down and dropping her head into her hands. "A few months ago everything was fine and we wanted the same things. Then suddenly he's changed his mind and we're going nowhere."

"Does he want to break up?" Claire asked.

"No, but I do. I told him I'm not going to wait around in a relationship that's a dead end, and he said I was being childish and unreasonable." She wiped her nose on the back of her hand before reaching for another tissue.

"Asshole," I hissed. "What did you say to that?"

"I said 'Go fuck yourself.'"

That made me grin a mile wide.

"But am I making a mistake?" Margot asked desperately. "I mean, I don't need a ring tomorrow, but I at least liked knowing we were building toward something. It made me feel happy and secure in the future. Now everything's just fucked!" She started weeping again.

I scooted closer and rubbed her back. "You did the right thing, Margot. A woman like you does *not* need to wait around for *any* man, least of all a dipshit like Tripp."

"I just kept thinking, if I don't do it now, he's just going to dump me later, once he's tired of me," she sobbed. "And I couldn't bear the thought that he'd be the one to call it off, and I'd look like the biggest fool on the planet, waiting around all these years for a proposal that never came."

"No one would ever say that," Claire said loyally.

"Yes, they would," Margot insisted. "You don't know how people talk in those circles. They're so nice to your face and so vicious behind your back. I bet they're already talking about me."

"Listen, posh people don't have a monopoly on shitty gossip," I told her. "They just do it more quietly in more expensive rooms. And everything is *not* fucked! The way I see it, your future is wide open now."

"I agree," said Claire. "And if love and marriage is what you want, you'll find it. I know you will."

"Or *fuck* love and marriage!" I said. "Get out there and do things you've always wanted to do! Take a trip, get a new job, change things up! Maybe this is a wake-up call."

She sniffed, looking at me with puffy eyes. "Maybe. Fucking hurts, though."

My heart squeezed as she dissolved into tears again. "I know. I'm sorry."

I called Quinn on the way home, who said he'd waited for me, and dinner would be ready when I got there. I apologized for being late, but he said apologies weren't necessary, a friend in need was more important than spaghetti, and besides, this gave him something to punish me for later.

God, he was so fucking perfect.

It was terrifying…what was I *doing*?

Seeing Margot come apart at the seams like that was making me wonder if I had any fucking clue. The last two weeks had been so intense—I hardly recognized myself. I wanted to be with Quinn almost all the time. I thought about him constantly. A few times, I even caught myself about to say *I love you*, before memory and common sense kicked in and reminded me what happened the last time I did that.

This was fucked up.

I didn't believe in love like that, did I? But then what was that feeling that stopped my heart and stole my breath, made me break all my rules and drop my defenses? That made me want to share things with him I'd never even thought about sharing with anyone else? What was that longing for him when we were apart? What was that flutter in my stomach when I saw him again? What was that tingle in my skin, that rush to the head, that certainty in my bones that when I was with him, nothing else mattered?

This couldn't happen.

It couldn't be me.

But when I walked into his flat and saw him in the kitchen putting together our dinner…when he looked over at me and his eyes lit up…when he stopped what he was doing and came over to kiss me…I knew I was drowning.

A sweat broke out on my back, and the room spun. My stomach churned and my head throbbed, my mouth was dry and my legs were weak.

This is why they call it lovesick.

I couldn't even breathe.

After he kissed me hello, he started talking about something, and his voice seemed to come at me from the end of a long tunnel. I heard sounds but not words. My body felt heavy, as if the force of gravity had just increased exponentially, and I braced a hand on the counter because I was afraid I wasn't strong enough to hold myself up.

I was in love with him.

I was in *love* with him.

How had I let this happen?

I had to fix this.

Now.

Good thing I had an emergency exit strategy all planned out. I always had.

I couldn't even taste the food. I could barely get it on my fork. I think I made conversation, but in the back of my mind I kept seeing Margot on the floor, hearing her pitiful sobs. I had to protect myself from that…I had to stick to what I knew was right for me, and that meant doing what I always said I'd do if I fell for someone.

It meant stepping back from Quinn.

But you'll miss him! screamed a voice in my head.

You'll miss the sex, you'll miss his jokes, you'll miss his voice, his face, his kindness. You'll miss his teasing and cooking and maybe even the cuddling. You'll miss the way he makes you feel.

No, I won't, I argued back. I might miss all those other things, but right now all I feel is terror. *I'm sorry that I have to sacrifice all those other things to feel safe again, but I do.*

So when he mentioned that he'd booked movers for Tuesday, I saw the opening and took it.

"Oh, good," I said, shocking even myself with how calm I sounded. *Yes. Stay cool. Make a joke.* "About time you got out of here."

He grinned. "I knew you'd be glad to get rid of me."

"Well, I wouldn't say *that*." I picked up my wine glass and hoped he didn't notice the way it trembled. "This has been really fun."

A quizzical look passed over his face. "Yeah. It has." A beat went by. "Isn't it still?"

I took a huge gulp of wine. "I guess so. I mean, with you moving out, it'll be harder to see each other."

"Uh huh…" His mind was working overtime, I could see it.

I dropped my eyes to my plate and pushed some pasta around. "And I've got a lot of big projects coming up at work."

"Really." He set his fork on the plate with a clink.

"Mmhm." *Oh God, oh God, don't look up.* I took a shaky breath. "So it's probably a good time to take a breather from all this anyway."

"All this what?"

I shrugged, feeling like I was stepping out onto the frozen lake, unsure how thin the ice was. One wrong step and I'd go under. "All this…time together. I won't have it anymore. And since you're moving out, it seems like the right decision."

"You're not making sense, Jaime." There was an edge to his tone. "What decision?"

Don't back down. This is the right thing. "To take a step back. Cool off. We were getting too serious anyway. And I'm not…good at that. I don't want it. So I think we should, you know, go back to what we said this was going to be. Friends that hang out every once in a while for fun."

Whew.

There. Got it out.

He said nothing, and I was dying to know what his expression was. Angry? Hurt? Shocked? What felt like a lifetime passed in uncomfortable silence. Finally, I couldn't resist looking up.

He was sitting back in the chair, arms crossed. And his face said *I know exactly what you're fucking doing.*

My first reaction was to bristle a little, even though he hadn't said a word. Did he think I was bluffing? That I'd back down? Well, I wouldn't! This wasn't a fucking game of chicken, this was *real* and it was my *heart* and my *life* and I couldn't give it away in the blind hope that things would work out. It was too scary, too unpredictable, too unbelievable. I didn't want to be dependent on anyone for anything! I was fine on my own! How dare he come into my life and turn it upside down this way! And why was he sitting there all silent and smoldering!? Didn't he fucking *care* that I was trying to break things off? He should care, because I was serious!

"Say something!" I finally blurted.

I swear to God, that fucker almost smiled.

"OK, Jaime. If that's what you want."

My jaw dropped. "Is that what you want?"

"No."

"Well...that's what I want." Fuck. *Fuck!* It's what I wanted, wasn't it? Why was his reaction throwing me off? Dammit, this was *just* like him!

"So you said." He stood up and carried his half-full plate into the kitchen. A few seconds later, I heard the faucet running and the sounds of dishes being rinsed and placed in the dishwasher.

I sat there at the table, feeling small and stubborn and angry and sad. Of all the reactions I'd thought he'd have, complaisance wasn't one of them. Was this some kind of trick? Reverse psychology? Did he think I'd change my mind and beg to take back my words? Well, I wouldn't. Pouting, I crossed my arms over my chest.

Then another thought occurred to me.

What if he really didn't care? What if he wasn't in love with me? What if I'd imagined all the deep, intense feelings between us? *Maybe I was just a game to him after all.*

The cynic in my head spoke up, the one that continued to shame me for breaking the rules and letting him in, the one that forced me to sleep in my own bed some nights. *You see? This validates everything. Of course you're a game! For fuck's sake,* love is a game—and no one plays fair. The only way to win it is *to get off the board.*

I believed the voice. But a tiny part of me wanted Quinn to fight back, to tell me I was wrong, to insist what we had was real and too good to throw away. Why wasn't he doing it?

He came into the dining room and reached for my plate. "Are you done?"

"Yes."

After he took it into the kitchen, I downed the last of my wine and followed him in. "So that's it, really? That's all you have to say?"

He didn't look at me, just kept loading the dishes. "What do you want me to say?"

That you love me, dammit.

Although, if he did…what would that change? Wouldn't that just make it worse? The problem here wasn't that we didn't feel the same about each other; it was that we *did*. And I couldn't handle it, so I'd just fucked everything up.

It was my last line of defense.

"Nothing," I snapped, irrationally angry with him for letting me walk out without a fight and furious with myself for being the kind of person who'd rather be alone than scared. Setting my empty wine glass on the counter with a clunk. "Nothing at all."

Fighting tears, I stormed out of his apartment, raced up to mine, and threw myself onto my bed, where I cried so hard I didn't even make a sound.

All this to avoid ending up like Margot, and yet that was exactly where I was—broken-hearted, mad, and desperately wondering if I'd done the right thing.

CHAPTER TWENTY-FIVE

Quinn

I couldn't sleep. All night long I lay there staring at the ceiling, cursing Jaime's stubborn streak and her fucked-up ideas about love and relationships.

Did she think I was stupid? Did she think I wouldn't see through her?

I *knew* her.

There was no way I'd misjudged her over the last six weeks—she didn't want to step back from us any more than I wanted to. It was fear, plain and simple. She was afraid of letting herself be happy with me. She saw her friend fall apart after a bad breakup, and it scared her. But rather than come to me and admit that, she'd run in the other direction. She couldn't handle her feelings for me, so she'd just decided to turn them off.

Well, she'd *try* to turn them off. But love wasn't like a fucking oven or faucet or lamp. There was no OFF switch. How was she planning to do it? She'd said something about being friends that occasionally hung out—and I was pretty sure by "hang out" she meant *fuck*—but there was no way I could do that.

Did she honestly think we could still have sex without feelings?

She wants to think that. She wants to believe that she's above falling for someone this way.

But she wasn't. I saw it in her face—she could hardly look at me while she was talking. And then she'd expected me to argue with her, as if that wouldn't just make her dig her heels in deeper. If I'd thought for one second that hearing me say "I love you, don't do this" would change her mind, I'd have said it.

But that wasn't the answer.

Jaime wasn't like any woman I knew. She didn't need me to declare my feelings—she knew how I felt. This really didn't have anything to do with me.

It was about her.

She had to get over her fear and her skepticism, and it was something she had to do on her own.

She had to miss me, miss what we had. More than that, she had to see it as something she didn't want to live without, something worth the risk. I knew she'd miss the sex, and fucking hell, I would too, but she had to miss more than that for her to change. She could get great sex from any guy with half a brain and a functional dick (although I do like to think mine is more than just functional). What *we* had was something special.

At least, I'd thought it was.

I'd tried hard to be what she wanted, give her the space she needed, respect her boundaries, but if it wasn't enough, then I'd have to get over her somehow. Move on. Try to forget.

The thought was like a sledgehammer to my chest.

I fucking *loved* her. I wanted to *be* with her. I didn't need her to be perfect or wear a ring or spend every waking moment with me, I just wanted to share my life with her, make her laugh, make her happy—and I wanted some assurance that she wasn't going to run away whenever she got scared.

I thought about the way my father had taken off on my mother and felt a rush of sympathy for her. Did I love a lost cause, too?

I knew one thing—I'd been wrong to think I could prove to her that love existed…she'd refuse to see it. She didn't *want* to see it. She wouldn't let herself.

And there wasn't a thing I could do about it.

I couldn't stay here any longer. Knowing she was up there, probably miserable and too stubborn to come down here and talk about it, would drive me crazy. I'd give in and go up to her, and we'd either end up fighting or fucking, neither of which would alter her point of view.

No. She'd turned me away, so I'd give her what she wanted.

No matter how much it hurt.

CHAPTER
TWENTY-SIX

Jaime

He moved out the next day.

Without a word to me.

He didn't call or text or leave a note or anything. He just packed up and left.

I realized this because I actually went down to talk to him after I got home from work. I'd spent the whole night crying and the entire day at work agonizing over what I'd done and his reaction to it. I wasn't even sure what I was going to say to him when I knocked on his door; I just knew that I hated where we'd left things, and I didn't want him to move out without at least one more conversation.

Maybe I'd been too hasty in calling things off. Maybe I'd let Margot's situation influence me too much. Maybe this time he'd try harder to change my mind.

I knew my face looked puffy and terrible—people at work kept asking if I'd had an allergic reaction to something—but I knocked anyway. When he didn't answer, I realized that I hadn't seen his car on the street. (Never did clean out the other half of the garage. Yet another thing to feel bad about.) I'm not sure what made me check the handle to see if the door was locked, but when the knob turned, I pushed it open.

I knew right away he was gone. It just felt empty. All the furniture was still there, obviously, but none of his things—no books on the coffee table, no boots by the door, no photos of him and his mom on the built-in shelves next to the fireplace.

Wandering into the kitchen, I noticed he'd left it spotless—no dishes in the sink or even in the dishwasher, no crumbs on the floor, no spills on the counter. I opened the fridge and saw that he'd emptied it out, and the freezer as well.

In his bedroom, I checked the closet and nightstand drawer. No condoms. The thought of Quinn needing condoms at his new place hit me hard in the gut, and I sat back on the bare mattress as if I'd been pushed.

But he's mine!

Fists and jaw clenched in rage, I went into the bathroom and opened all the drawers, even peeked into the shower. Everything was gone, but I could still smell his soap and cologne.

Goddamn it!

I ran back through his flat, slammed the door, and pounded up the steps. Inside my apartment, I threw myself on the couch and curled into a ball, hugging a throw pillow to my stomach.

He must have called the movers and rescheduled for today. But why? He hadn't even seemed upset last night! Was this just to punish me? Make me regret my decision?

Or maybe overnight he'd decided I was right, and stepping back was the best thing for us. Maybe I wasn't worth the hassle.

Angry and confused, I spent a wretched hour staring at my phone, even picking it up once and nearly pressing his name, but I never reached out.

I endured another miserable night.

Followed by a miserable week.

And then another.

I even called Alex, hoping he might drop Quinn's name, but he didn't.

I thought about him every day, endless questions peppering my brain all day long. What was he doing? Did he miss me? Was he settling in OK? How was the view of Comerica Park? Who would he take to Opening Day? Had he slept with anyone? Was he thinking about me? Who did he talk to about his mom? Who did he tease? Who did he cook for?

His Instagram posting had stopped, too.

Damn him! It was like he knew I was trying to stalk him and he was thwarting my efforts!

My body craved his with such intensity, even my vibrator didn't take the edge off. My heart ached painfully when I thought about never being close to him again.

You were always going to feel like this, said the cynic in me. *So it's now instead of later, big deal. In fact, better now than later, because more time together would have meant even stronger feelings, right? It would have been harder down the road. When there's a matter to be settled, you settle it.*

Yes! I clung to that. It made sense to me.

My friends? Not so much.

"You did *what*?" Claire screeched at GNO, three days after I broke up with Quinn.

"I broke things off with Quinn. It was time." I couldn't look either one of them in the eye so I focused on my martini.

"What do you mean, 'It was time?'" Margot said suspiciously. "Was there some sort of expiration date?"

"No. It was just…time to step back. You know me." I shrugged, trying to sound casual. It felt horrible to lie to my friends, but I thought if I could convince them I was OK, I'd have a better chance of convincing myself.

It was not going well.

Claire's jaw was open and cocked to one side, eyes narrowed. Margot was making this face she makes with one eyebrow up, lips pressed together, her gaze so searing hot you'd swear she could fry an egg with it.

(Tonight the role of the egg will be played by Jaime Owens.)

"This is bullshit, Jaime," she said. "This is just you freaking out because someone finally *got* to you."

"Exactly," said Claire. "Quinn is crazy about you, and you're crazy about him. I've seen it."

"That doesn't mean anything," I said lamely. "And I'm not *that* crazy about him."

"Don't lie to us. We've known you too long, and your cheeks get too red." Claire shook her head. "You're sabotaging this on purpose."

"I am not!"

"You are, but let's ignore that for a second." Margot waved a hand in the air. "What did Quinn say when you said you wanted to break up?"

"He didn't even care."

"Another lie," said Margot.

"Yep," said Claire.

"It's not! He didn't say anything, and when I told him he had to say *something*, he said, 'OK, if that's what you want.'" I left out the part where he said it wasn't what he wanted. Didn't really fit into the Poor Me picture I was painting.

Margot sat back, arms crossed. "I don't buy it."

Claire shook her head. "Me either."

"Look, you guys can gang up on me all you want, but that doesn't change the fact that Quinn moved out without saying *anything* to me the very next day. I'm telling you, he *didn't care*. Now can we please talk about something else? I'm trying to forget the whole thing."

Their faces softened.

"Sorry, Jaims. We're not trying to gang up on you." Margot put her hand on my arm. "We just don't want to see you hurt."

"I'm looking out for myself so I *don't* get hurt, OK?" I said, trying to force the lump in my throat to go away. "You of all people should understand me right now."

She didn't say anything, but she nodded and patted my arm. "OK. Let's talk about something else."

"How are *you* doing, Margot?" Claire asked her.

She took a breath. "Better. Not great, but better. Thinking things through. Talking to my therapist. I think you might have been right about a change, Jaime."

I smiled, glad to hear I was right about something.

Maybe I wouldn't cry myself to sleep tonight.

Alex's birthday was toward the end of March, and Nolan was throwing him a party at their house. I had to show my face, but I was terrified of running into Quinn. We hadn't seen or spoken to each other in three weeks, and I was finally able to go a day without crying or eating a king-sized Hershey bar, but I wasn't anywhere near over him. Would seeing him again fuck me up completely? Would I fall apart?

No. Don't let it. Be strong.

Figuring strength would come easier if I felt good about my appearance, I got my eyebrows waxed and my hair blown out. I wore what I considered my best armor, a sexy little black dress that showed off my curves and the leopard heels. I gave myself a Sophia Loren eye and a classic red lip. When I saw the necklace he'd given me in my jewelry drawer, my stomach twisted. I loved it so much, but I hadn't been able to bring myself to wear it since Quinn moved out. The reminder of that amazing night was too painful, so I left it in the drawer and chose a gold tassel pendant instead.

At the party, I had a cocktail to calm my nerves, and then another one after that because Quinn hadn't arrived yet but I knew he had to be coming. By the bottom of the second drink, I still hadn't seen him, so I approached Nolan. "Hey, was Quinn invited?"

"Yes," he said, opening a bottle of red. "But he said he was going to be a little late."

"Oh," I said, hoping I sounded as if I didn't care. "Just wondering. Hey, can you pour me a glass of that?"

Twenty minutes later, I was sipping wine in one corner of the living room, watching the doorway like a bird of prey, when he walked in.

My heart stopped.

The room spun.

I'd forgotten how beautiful he was.

As if he had radar where I was concerned, his eyes found me immediately. I wanted to look away, but I couldn't. I wanted to breathe, but I couldn't. I wanted to run over to him and wrap my legs around his waist, but I couldn't. The room seemed to go silent, the air full of something so thick it stifled the sound. My mouth was dry. I lifted my glass to my lips and drank, barely tasting the wine.

God, what had I done? Why had I walked away from him? What the hell was wrong with me? Physical need for him took over my senses.

I have to get him back in my bed, in my arms, in my body.

But how could I do it? Was he still mad? Would he even come over to say hi?

I decided to try a little smile.

He nodded without smiling back, and went into the kitchen.

Fuck! Why had I smiled at him? Now I seemed weak and pathetic, and I didn't want to come from that position. I needed to find a conversation to get in on before he came back in here and saw me standing alone. Searching the room, I saw Alex talking to some of his friends from work, and made my way over to them. I positioned myself so I'd see if Quinn came into he living room, but he never did.

Goddamn him! Was he made of steel or something? How could he ignore me like this?

Because he doesn't care.

I bit my lip. Was that true? Had he gotten over me already? I couldn't bear the thought. I downed the last of my wine and went for more, stumbling a little on my way out of the room.

From the kitchen, I could see into the family room, where Quinn was talking to Nolan and a woman I didn't recognize. Jealousy made my nostrils flare. I poured another glass of pinot noir, spilling some on the counter.

When I looked up again, I caught him staring at me.

You do care, Quinn. I feel it. And I want you—I need to feel your hands on me, hear you whisper dirty words, watch your face as you come.

Suddenly I had an idea—the perfect plan for seduction.

It was risky, but if it worked it would be kind of funny, and Quinn loved a good joke. Plus sales pitches were my thing, right? I was a little drunk, but I thought I knew what Quinn wanted to hear—the three little words that would lure him into my bed.

It would totally go my way this time.

Tossing my hair over my shoulder, I headed in his direction.

CHAPTER TWENTY-SEVEN

Quinn

God, she was gorgeous. That dress she was wearing clung to every curve. Fuck, I missed those curves. And her hair. I missed the way it felt in my hands, the way it smelled, the way it looked spilling across the pillow. Those shoes were the ones she'd been wearing the night I took her to The Whitney, the night she'd asked me to stay over, the night of the Finger.

My cock jumped, and I stifled a groan.

I'd known she would be here tonight, and I almost hadn't come, but hiding out wasn't my style. Then when I saw her, standing there in the living room by herself, looking so beautiful, so vulnerable, I nearly lost it and ran right for her. Not a day went by that I didn't want her back.

But not on her terms, and not with her boundaries. I wanted more.

She walked up to me, and I could tell right away she was tipsy. Her eyes were glassy, and she didn't seem too steady on her feet. "Excuse me," I said to Nolan and the woman he'd introduced me to (although I'd forgotten her name instantly). Moving away from them slightly, I turned to Jaime.

"Hi," she said, so friendly it was as if she'd forgotten she broke up with me three weeks ago.

"Hi."

Suddenly she took me by the arm and pulled me into the hallway, past the kitchen, and into the bathroom. She let go of my arm and shut the door, setting her wine glass on the vanity. The light was off but a huge green candle with three wicks had been lit by the sink.

"I'm so glad you're here." She moved closer, pressing her chest to mine and running a hand up my lapel. "I missed you. You left without saying goodbye." She had lipstick on her teeth.

"Are you OK?" I asked her, feeling the way she swayed toward me.

"I'm totally fine," she said. "Mmmm, you smell good."

"How did you get here?"

"I drove." She toyed with the collar of my shirt. "Why, do you want to take me home?"

"I want to make sure you get home safely."

She giggled. "You're worried about me. I like it. And look where we are."

I looked around. "The bathroom?"

More laughter. "Yes. I want a do-over."

It hit me right as she spoke what she was doing.

"I think I love you, Quinn."

Oh, Jesus. "Jaime."

"I want you back."

"Back where?"

"With me. In my bed."

"Why?"

"Because I miss you there."

I stared down at her, searching her face for the truth, for some evidence that she knew what she was saying to me, for some sign of change in her.

I didn't see any of it.

"No." It was hard keeping my hands to myself the way she was hanging on me, but I did, one clenched around a beer bottle, one fisted at my side.

"What?" She blinked.

"Why are you doing this, Jaime?"

"I told you," she said, one hand sliding down the front of my jeans, the other snaking around my waist. "I want you. I want back what we had."

"Why did you throw it away? Be honest this time."

She lifted her shoulders, her focus on my chest. "I was just being silly."

I set my beer down and gently pushed her away, holding her forearms out in front of me, forcing her to look me in the eye. "Answer the question, Jaime. I deserve the truth from you."

"You know why."

"Say it."

"Because I was scared, OK?" She stepped back, knotting her fingers at her waist. "I'm scared of the way I feel. I'm scared that when things fall apart, I will too. And they always fall apart, Quinn."

"Bullshit."

"Excuse me?"

"You're not scared it will fall apart. You're scared it won't."

"What do you mean?" Her voice shook.

"You hide behind this 'love is just a fairy tale used to sell lipstick' wall so you don't have to make yourself vulnerable to another person. So you don't have to trust someone and let him trust you. So you don't have to fucking commit to someone and be willing to say I'm sorry or I forgive you or help me or I need you. So you don't have to be humbled by a feeling so fucking strong it changes your life. Well, I want that. I want to trust you. I want to need you. I *want* to be humbled by love, because it makes me feel alive and part of something good."

"What we *had* was good! Why can't we go back to it?"

I shook my head. "Because I changed my mind. I'm in love with you, but I want *more*. I want a commitment from you, a future with you, not just a fling. I want to hear you say you believe it's possible."

"That is what I'm saying, isn't it?" she asked, but I heard the doubt in her voice.

"No, what you're saying is that you want me back in your bed, because the sex is fun and you miss what we had, but it's just temporary because these feelings won't last."

"But I said I love you! Isn't that enough?"

"Those are pretty words, Jaime, but right now it sounds to me like you're using them as means to an end. That isn't love."

"You think I'm lying to you?"

"No. I think you're lying to yourself. I think you want more too, and you're scared to take it."

She went silent, her shoulders slumping.

"You're right about serious relationships not being all hearts and flowers and orgasms, Jaime. That's *falling* in love. Over time, it's not that anymore. It takes *work*. It takes trust and sacrifice and faith in something you can't see. It means sticking the fuck around when you're scared or tempted or angry. It's knowing that someone has your back and will be there at the end of your best days and your worst. It's understanding that you're part of something bigger than yourself, and fighting for it. I know it's rare." I softened my voice. "But that's what I'm looking for. And life is short."

She started to cry. "I don't know what to do. I'm miserable without you, but I don't think I'm capable of being what you want."

You are. You just refuse to see it.

My chest hurt, and my gut was in knots. I wanted to hold her so badly, but I couldn't give in, and I wasn't going to argue with her. "If that's the truth, then let me go."

After a long pause, she stepped aside. I opened the door and shouldered by her without looking back.

I went right to Alex. "Listen, I have to go, but don't let your sister drive home tonight. Get her a ride or keep her here. She's been drinking a lot."

"OK." He looked concerned. "Everything alright?"

"I don't know." The truth was, I felt like fucking overturning the coffee table, maybe throwing it through the front windows.

"Let's hang out this week, OK? I'll make sure Jaime gets home safely or stays over."

"Sounds good." I shook his hand and he pulled me in for a hug. "Thanks."

I let myself out and walked to my car with long, angry strides. What the fuck was I supposed to do with her? *I think I love you?* Did she really think I was just looking for the words? It wasn't that hearing them from her hadn't made me happy—it had.

But it wasn't enough.

CHAPTER
TWENTY-EIGHT

Jaime

My eyelids felt like stubborn garage doors, but I managed to get them open after a few tries.

Oh, God.

The room wasn't bright, but even the small amount of sun creeping through the blinds stabbed my retinas like a thousand daggers. My head was…not good.

Slowly, I sat up and looked around. Someone had put me in a guest room at Alex and Nolan's house, or I'd put myself in here—I couldn't remember. I was still wearing my dress, and my heels were on the floor.

Somehow I managed to hobble over to them, lean down, and pick them up, but the room was not cooperating. The floor pitched at strange angles and the walls appeared to be circling me.

I made it to the bathroom, where I thought I might throw up, but I didn't. Then I thought about flushing myself down the toilet, but since that wasn't an option, I used the bathroom, washed my hands, and splashed cold water on my face

Then I looked in the mirror.

MISTAKE.

I looked almost as bad as I felt. The carefully applied cat's-eye liner had morphed into raccoon eyes. My face was pale, my eyes were bloodshot, and my matted hair made Margot's blond bird nests look like gold satin. The effect of two cocktails and many, many glasses of red wine was not pretty.

"Whyyyyy," I moaned.

But I knew why—to dull the pain.

When I thought about what had happened with Quinn, I felt the sharp sting of it poking through the haze of my hangover.

But I deserved it.

I'd fucked up.

Again.

It had seemed like such a good idea, cornering him in the bathroom, such a cute nod to our past, but then nothing had come out right.

Because I'm not good at that stuff. I don't know how to do it.

Frowning at my reflection one last time, I made my way downstairs, carrying my shoes in one hand and my dignity in the other.

Nolan and Alex were bright-eyed and chipper, having coffee and muffins in the kitchen.

"There she is!" Nolan hopped up and grabbed a big glass from a cupboard, filling it with water. "You're gonna want this, sunshine. I'll get you some coffee and ibuprofen too."

"Thanks," I said weakly. My tongue felt like it had a fur coat on.

"How are you doing?" Alex grinned at me from over the rim of his cup.

"Don't ask. Ugh." I grimaced as I sat down at the kitchen table. "I think there's a dead rodent in my mouth."

Nolan set the water and ibuprofen in front of me and I tried to smile. "Thanks."

"Want to talk about it?" my brother asked.

I swallowed the pills and some water before answering. "I don't know what to say."

"Quinn was worried about you."

I sighed.

"What happened with that?" Nolan wondered, setting a cup of coffee in front of me before sitting down again.

"What happened was that I blew it about three weeks ago. And then I blew it again last night."

"How so?"

I inhaled and exhaled. Even breathing hurt. "I saw what a bad breakup did to Margot, and I panicked that my feelings for Quinn were getting too serious."

"Too serious for what?" Alex asked.

"For comfort." I tried a sip of the coffee. "You know how I am."

"So what did you do?" Nolan pressed. "Break it off?"

"Yes. But I was fucking miserable without him, so last night when I saw him, I had this brilliant idea that I could get him back—and it didn't work."

"What did you do?" Alex questioned.

"I told him I loved him, because I thought that's what he needed to hear."

"Did you say it like that?" Nolan asked.

"Like what?"

"Like you were only saying it, not feeling it."

"Jesus!" I set my coffee cup down with a thud, some of it sloshing over the side. "What is with you people? I do feel it, OK? I *love* him. Am I supposed to sing it? Cry tears of joy? Shoot a rainbow out of my ass? That's just not me." I went over to the counter to get some paper towel.

"No, I don't think you need to do any of those things," Nolan said. "I just think you need to say it because you mean it, not because it's what he wants to hear. What was his reaction?"

"He said he didn't believe me. No, wait." As I mopped up the spill, I tried to think back to what his words had been. My memory was foggy. "I don't think he said he didn't believe me. He said I was lying, but not to him. To myself."

"About what?" Alex asked.

I focused on my hands. "About…about the reason I pulled away from him. He said it wasn't because I was scared we wouldn't last; it's because I'm scared we *would*."

"And are you?"

"I don't know." Now I was lying to them too. "Maybe."

"Why would that scare you?" Nolan looked at me like I was one of his patients. Sometimes it was really annoying that he was a therapist and so good at sussing out the truth behind feelings.

"Because I'll fuck it up!" I burst out, surprising even myself. "It's inevitable. And he deserves better."

Alex looked a little shocked, but Nolan barely reacted. "So it will be *you* that hurts *him*?"

"Maybe," I said, fighting tears and nausea. "I mean, not on purpose. But he kept talking about all these things that love involves—trust and apologies and fights and forgiveness and sacrifice—I mean, what if I don't have it in me?"

"Don't you think you do?"

"OK, enough with the therapy-speak." I threw the soaked paper towel away and sat down again. "I get what you're trying to do, but the thing is, there are no for-sure answers to these questions."

"You're right," Alex said quietly. "There aren't."

We both looked at him.

"Then what's the secret? Tell me, *please*. How do you make promises to someone when you don't know what the future holds?"

Alex shrugged. "There is no secret. There is no magic, Jaime. No way to tell what the future looks like. The point is that you're willing to take the chance anyway. You're willing to say, I don't know what's going to happen, but I know I want you with me on this journey."

"Exactly," agreed Nolan. "It's not as if Alex and I know something you don't. We love each other and work hard at this. And he was just as reluctant as you are to commit to forever."

"You were?" I looked at my brother, surprised.

"At first, I was," said Alex. "I never wanted to be married. I thought, 'What's the point?' We'll just end up hating each other. Doesn't everyone?"

"Yes! So how did you get over that?" I propped my heavy, aching head in my hand.

"I weighed my feelings for him against my fears, and in the end, I decided what scared me most was the thought of a life without him."

Nolan reached out and took his hand. "Oh honey, that's so sweet. Does that mean we can have the doves?"

"No," Alex said firmly. "No doves."

Nolan sighed. "Anyway, Jaime, does that help at all?"

"I guess so. I mean, seeing how happy you guys are makes me think maybe there's a chance for me, but…" I took a breath. "I have to figure out how to open myself up to it. I've guarded against it so long that it feels like I'm trying to get in the game when I've been skipping practice."

"Ask yourself the hard questions, and don't be afraid of the answers," Alex said. "Remember we are not our parents. Be open to every possibility. That's my advice."

"It's good advice." Nolan patted his hand. "And you know, Jaime, there's no shame in talking to a therapist about this stuff. Not me, of course, but I can give you a name of someone I think would be good for you."

"Thanks, I think that might be a good idea. And thanks for letting me crash here. I definitely drank too much."

"Happens to everyone. Just don't let it happen at the wedding," Alex warned. "I'm not dragging your sorry ass home that night."

I smiled. "You won't have to."

"And maybe find a different hairstylist." Nolan wrinkled his nose and waved a hand at my head. "The whole grunge thing isn't really working for you."

I threw a muffin at him. But I felt a little bit better.

In the next week, I did a lot of soul searching. I made an appointment with the therapist Nolan recommended, a woman named Jenna, who helped me sift through my feelings. We talked a lot that first session about my childhood and how my mom and dad's marriage and parenting style had affected me. She felt that those things had had a bigger impact on me than I realized, and after talking about it, I agreed.

After hearing me talk for a solid hour, she wasn't at all surprised to learn that I'd been reluctant to fall in love. She gave me some more things to think about, additional questions to ask myself, and I made an appointment for the following week.

I saw Margot and Claire that night, and they told me how proud they were.

"I think it's wonderful you're seeing a therapist," Margot said. "I love mine."

"You're doing the right thing," Claire agreed. "Have you come to any conclusions?"

I took a deep breath. "I miss him like crazy and I love him."

Claire shook her head. "Never thought I'd see the day."

"What about the things he wants?" Margot asked. I think she understood where he was coming from even better than I did. "Can you handle it?"

"I think I can," I said. "I have no idea what kind of girlfriend I'll be, but I can't bear the thought of him with anyone else or being with anyone else myself, so if he wants a girlfriend, it's gonna be me."

They grinned. "When are you going to talk to him?" asked Claire.

"Soon. Maybe this weekend." I made a face. "But I have to work up my nerve. Twice now I've told this man I love him, and it ended badly both times."

"Third time's the charm," Margot said confidently.

I really hoped she was right.

The next day, I texted him. **Hey, can we talk?**

He didn't answer for hours, and when he did, it was disappointing. **In London for a shoot. Home on the 7th. Unless you want to talk on the phone.**

The 7th…my heart sank. **So you'll miss the wedding?**

Unfortunately, yes. Scheduling mixup. I talked to Alex about it.

OK. Get in touch when you're back?

I will.

I set my phone next to me on the couch and stared at it, my bottom lip caught between my teeth. It was hard to believe I hadn't wanted to go to the wedding with him when he'd first asked. Now I was devastated he'd miss it.

At least he wouldn't have to suffer through my toast. I was still struggling to put it together, although something Alex had said the morning after his birthday had been buzzing around in my brain ever since.

There is no magic.

And I knew what he'd meant—I'd been saying the same thing for years.

But now…I was going to disagree.

CHAPTER TWENTY-NINE

Jaime

Alex and Nolan's wedding day dawned clear, bright, and crisp. I woke up in a surprisingly good mood, considering I'd been dreading making the toast for a year and Quinn wouldn't be there tonight to get me through it. But I felt optimistic about both my words and the evening ahead—and I was genuinely happy for Alex and Nolan. I had a new appreciation for their relationship.

After breakfast I took a walk, breathing in the cool spring air and going over my little speech in my head again and again.

I spent the late morning and early afternoon at the salon and then dressing in my old bedroom at my parents' house, where the car would pick us up. Getting ready in my old bathroom reminded me of being a teenager—and crushing on Quinn, of course. *Who'd have thought, after all this time, he'd be the love of my life?*

The thought gave me shivers.

Since I was the only female attendant, I'd gotten to pick my own outfit, and I'd chosen a gorgeous light gray dress that coordinated with the grooms' charcoal gray suits. (Light gray was on the list of Approved Wardrobe Colors Nolan had given family to guide their choice of wedding attire.)

I wore diamond earrings, borrowed from Margot, and the necklace Quinn had given me, and I had my hair done up in a twist, which showed off the jewelry and the cutout in the back of the dress.

Both the ceremony and reception were held at the Ford Piquette Avenue Plant, which sounds like a crazy place to hold a wedding, but I had to hand it to Nolan—the place looked fantastic. It was the perfect spot.

The industrial elements—Model T's parked along the room's perimeter, the exposed brick on the walls and ductwork on the ceiling, the huge factory windows, the wood-planked floor—gave it a rustic, masculine feeling. The flowers, linens and party lights lent softer elegance, and the fading sun cast the entire room in pale amber light. Almost two hundred guests were seated in rows of white folding chairs.

A string quartet played as our parents and Nolan's were seated, then Nolan's brother Sean took my arm and we walked up the aisle together. Once we'd reached the officiant, we split to each side, just as we'd rehearsed the previous night.

When I turned to face the back of the room, I saw him

Quinn.

He'd snuck in somehow, and he was standing at the back, dressed in a dark suit and looking so handsome he took my breath away. My flowers jittered in my hands.

He's here! He came!

A moment later, Alex and Nolan were walking up the aisle hand in hand, and I found myself completely choked up. They looked so happy, so in love, so sure of themselves. I thought about what it had taken for them to get here—as a gay couple, getting married wasn't something they took for granted—and I felt lucky to witness it.

I peeked out at Quinn. He smiled at me—not huge, but it made my heart pound all the same. I started thinking about what I was going to say to him and realized I was totally unprepared.

Damn it! How dare he surprise me like this! I wanted to get it right this time, and I hadn't practiced!

OK, no panicking. Maybe it will be even better if it's unrehearsed…just say what you're feeling without holding back.

When the grooms kissed to seal their union, my eyes filled, and my heart thumped with joy. When they embraced each other and I saw the tears on Nolan's face, I gave up trying to stem the tide, and let mine fall too.

Love was real, and it was worth celebrating.

I only had a few minutes between the ceremony and the elaborate photo shoot Nolan had planned, and I had to use most of it to repair my eye makeup, but I was dying to get to Quinn. After I touched up my face in the bathroom, I hurried back into the reception room, where guests were mingling with drinks in their hands, talking and listening to live jazz. My eyes skimmed the crowd, but I didn't see him right away.

A hand touched my shoulder. "Jaime."

I turned, and at the nearness of him, my breath caught. Without thinking, I threw my arms around his neck and hugged him tight. "Oh my God! What are you doing here?"

"I rearranged a few things. I actually have to fly back to London tomorrow night."

Surprised, I stepped back. "You do? When did you fly in?"

"Today."

"You flew in for one night?"

"I wanted to be here."

I smiled. "Alex will be so happy."

"It wasn't all for Alex," he said quietly. "I wanted to see you too. You look gorgeous."

"Thank you."

"You're wearing the necklace."

"Of course I am." As I touched the circle pendant, I heard my name being called and looked over to see the coordinator gesturing for me to come with her. "Crap. I have to go take pictures. But I want to talk to you."

"It's OK. I'm not going anywhere."

"Good. I'm not either." Impulsively, I took his face in my hands and kissed him full on the lips. "I mean it, Quinn. I'm here, I'm yours, I love you, and I want this for us."

"You do?" Grinning, he looked around. "All this?"

I wrinkled my nose. "Maybe not the two hundred people." *Deep breath.* "But lately I've been really inspired by Alex and Nolan, and I've been thinking a lot about what you said about falling in love, and staying in it."

"Yeah?"

"Yeah. You were right—I didn't let myself believe in love, because I was scared to give someone else that kind of power over me, and I've never been very good at sharing myself with anyone. It seemed so much easier to dismiss it as fiction."

"It is easier."

"But I don't want to do that anymore. I need you in my life." I heard my name being called again. "Gah. Too much going on at once."

"It's OK." He kissed my forehead. "I understand."

"I have to go outside. Wait for me here?"

"As long as it takes."

I smiled at him before hurrying toward the exit, my heart pounding as quickly as my heels on the wood.

CHAPTER THIRTY

Quinn

While Jaime was gone, I had a drink and chatted with a couple high school friends, but my mind was completely focused on her. She looked and sounded so *different*. I mean, she looked beautiful, like she always did, but her expression when she told me she loved me was so guileless and natural. I heard nothing false in her voice, saw no lie in her eyes. Prior to tonight, the only other times I'd seen her look that open and honest was during sex.

It was such a fucking relief.

While in London, I'd second-guessed myself a thousand times for walking away from her at Alex's party. *You asshole, you love her! Why do you have to be so hard on her?* I felt like I owed her an apology for that. But in the end, I always came to the same conclusion—if she was going to remain closed off to the possibility of a future, if she was truly only in this for the fun of it, if she was the kind of person who would leave whenever she felt threatened by her feelings or mine…I couldn't be with her.

But I'd missed her. And every night, I hoped what I'd said was getting through to her, and she just needed time.

When she'd texted me that she wanted to talk, I couldn't wait to get home and find out.

Thankfully, the photographer I was shooting with in London felt bad enough about the scheduling mix-up that she agreed to finish up on Monday instead of today, which was how I'd been able to take the quick trip. It would be terrible having to leave again tomorrow, but at least this time, I'd know I was coming home to something good.

Something beautiful, I thought as Jaime entered the room and walked toward me. *Something that matters to me.*

"Hey," she said as I kissed her cheek.

"Hey. Have I told you how fucking spectacular you look in that dress?"

She laughed. "Maybe. But you can keep telling me."

I slipped an arm around her waist and spoke in her ear. "You look fucking spectacular in that dress, but I think it will look even *more* spectacular on my new bedroom floor. Let's go find out."

"Mmm, I like the sound of that but I think my brother would kill me if I left before the big toast."

"That's right." I let go of her and studied her face. "Are you nervous?"

She tilted a hand side to side, fingers stretched. "A bit. I mean, I know what I want to say. I just hope I get through it."

"You will. I have faith." People had begun sitting down for dinner, but there were some things I wanted to say to her before I went to my table. "Listen, I want to apologize for the way I treated you at Alex's that night. I was hard on you."

"You were," she agreed. "But those were things I needed to hear, so no apology necessary. If you'd been sweet about it, I probably wouldn't have taken them to heart. I needed the hard words."

I gave her my best smolder. "I have lots of hard things for you. Not just words."

"So thoughtful," she said before slapping my arm. "Now stop trying to distract me with your dick when I'm supposed to be composing myself to speak in front of this crowd. You're riling me up."

"Sorry not sorry. And you were the one who brought up hard things, not me. I was just trying to apologize. But if you won't let me do that, then let me do this." I wrapped her up in my arms and pulled her close. "I know you don't love hugging in public and I'll let you go in a moment, but I need to hold you and tell you how much it means to me that you changed your mind about us."

"Quinn, don't."

I froze. "Don't?"

Her arms tightened around my waist. "Don't let me go."

∬

Lucky for me, there was an empty seat at the table where Jaime was sitting with Alex and Nolan, Sean and his wife, and another couple I recognized from Alex's birthday. The staff set a place for me, and Jaime held my hand under the table as the champagne was poured and someone handed a microphone to Nolan.

He stood, and the room hushed. "Thank you all for being here with us tonight. It means so much to Alex and me to see so many friends and family here celebrating together. One of the first things Alex told me about himself was how close he was to his sister, and I'm proud to call her *my* sister now, too." He looked at Jaime, and she smiled back, touching her hand to her heart. "She's agreed to kick off tonight's reception by saying a few words, so I'll turn the mic over to her for a toast."

I squeezed Jaime's hand before letting it go, and she stood up, smoothed her dress, and took the mic from Nolan.

"Thank you, Nolan, for the sweet introduction. Some girls might grow up wishing they had a baby sister, but not me. I've always thought another brother would be awesome, and I'm glad it's you. Love you both."

The crowd awwww'd collectively, and she smiled again at the grooms before turning toward the guests.

"For the last year, ever since Alex and Nolan asked me to make this toast, I've been panicking about it. What could I say about love and life that would mean something to them…" She glanced at the grooms. "And to you. Should I quote The Bard? The Bible? The Beatles?"

I grinned and she gave me a quick wink.

"I hunted around for the perfect lines, hoping to unearth something brilliant and beautiful, words that would unlock the mystery of love to a skeptic like me. Surely there was a secret to be discovered and shared." She paused. "But I couldn't find it. Nothing resonated. Nothing rang true. Love was just as mysterious as ever. So mysterious that I finally broke down and asked my big brother, '*What's the secret*?' Because when you look at these two…" She gestured toward Alex and Nolan. "You know that they know it."

After a pause, she went on. "And my brother said to me, 'Jaime, there is no secret. There is no magic. There is no way to know what the future holds. The point is that you're willing to take a chance.'" She took a breath. "I thought a lot about that in the following days. And I realized he was right—love isn't a secret to be unlocked, or a mystery to be solved. And marriage isn't the mystical union of two souls whose fate is written in the stars." Her voice got stronger. "It's a feeling, followed by a choice made in the face of chaos and uncertainty: I don't know where this road will take me, but I want you by my side on the journey." She glanced at me briefly, and my body warmed. "It's a leap of faith, and what a privilege it was to be here today and watch these two make it."

Smiling, she went on. "I *am* going to disagree slightly, though—what kind of kid sister would I be if I didn't?" She waited until the chuckling died down and turned to Alex and Nolan. "There is magic in a love like yours. Not the kind that can be seen or touched or explained, but the kind a person can feel when they look at you together. The kind that makes a person believe."

She paused for a moment, glanced at me, and then turned back to the crowd. "To Alex and Nolan—may the rest of their journey be as beautiful as their leap was today, and may we all be there to witness it!"

"To Alex and Nolan!" someone echoed, followed by a chorus of well wishes throughout the room.

I picked up my champagne and drank, so proud of Jaime I was bursting with it, and so in love with her I could hardly sit still. I watched as she went around the table to the grooms, hugging and kissing each of them, lingering a long time in Alex's arms. After giving the mic back to the band's vocalist, she returned to her chair, which I pulled out for her. Once I sat down again, I took her face in my hands and kissed her hard on the lips.

She looked relieved. "Oh my God, I'm glad that's over. How did I do? Too much Cheez Whiz?"

"Not nearly. You were great. It was beautiful and heartfelt."

"Thanks."

"So you're really a believer now, huh?"

That earned me a coy smile and playful lift of her shoulders. "Maybe."

"I'll take it." I planted a kiss on her nose. "Love bug."

She gave me a horrified look and scooted her chair away from me, making me grin from ear to ear.

She might believe in love, but she was still my Jaime—fire and ice all at once.

I wouldn't trade that for anything.

Later in the night, after dinner was over and the cake had been cut and Alex and Nolan had danced for the first time as a married couple, I was wondering how much longer Jaime wanted to stay when I heard the opening bars to a familiar tune.

She was sitting on my lap—her idea, not mine—and she grinned at me over one shoulder. "Is this your song?"

Chills swept down my arms as I heard the vocalist start to sing. "Who knows how long I've loved you? You know I love you still…"

"You remembered."

"Of course I did. I remember everything about you."

A rush of affection for her made my heart beat quicker. "Did you ask the band to play it?"

She nodded. "I'm not much of a singer, unfortunately, but if you'd like to dance, I'm game."

I stood, carefully setting her on her feet and taking her hand. On the dance floor, she melted into my arms, and I held her close, breathing in the sweet scent of her perfume. I listened to the words my mother used to sing and wished she were here, hoped she would be proud of me, missed her presence in my life. "She'd have loved this, you know. You and I together."

"Your mom?"

"Yes."

"That makes me happy."

"Me too."

She laid her head on my shoulder. "This is the longest I've ever stayed at a wedding. I usually bail by now."

"Does that mean you're having fun?"

"Yes. But being this close to you makes me want to go have fun somewhere else now."

"How about my place? Would you like to see it?"

"Yes," she said emphatically. "I've been dying to see it."

The song ended and we applauded before heading over to Alex and Nolan to say goodbye. They scolded us for leaving so early but looked happy to see us leaving together.

"Thanks again for the toast, sweet pea." Alex grabbed her in a quick hug. "It meant a lot to us."

"You're welcome," she said. "I know it was a little icky sweet, but I did mean what I said."

"Of course you did." I put my arm around her. "I think this is the start of a whole new icky sweet you."

I got the dagger eyes in return. "Don't start."

CHAPTER
THIRTY-ONE

Jaime

"Quinn, it's beautiful." I turned around inside his cavernous living room, taking in the high ceilings, shiny wood floors, brick walls, and huge windows. His furniture was modern and masculine with a touch of traditional—brown leather couches, an Eames chair, an antique bookcase. "And look at that view." I walked over to the window and looked out.

"Incredible, right?" He switched off the lights. "It's even better in the dark."

I laughed. "What isn't?"

He came up behind me and wrapped his arms around my waist, burying his face in my neck. It was the kind of embrace I'd have squirmed out of with anyone else, or maybe even just a few months ago with him.

Now I liked the closeness I felt when he held me. I liked feeling his body against mine even with our clothes on, not even knowing whether it would lead to sex.

But it had damn well better.

It had been too long, and we'd been looking at each other too hungrily all night, and a separation—however brief—loomed ahead.

Quinn kissed my throat, swept his tongue over my skin. "I love you so much. I'm so glad you're here."

I never thought those words would make me happy, but now I wanted to wrap myself up in them, roll around in them, drown in them.

"Me too." I tilted my head to the side, feeling the tingle begin between my legs. When I felt the nudge of his swelling cock against my ass, I reached behind me and rubbed my hand over it. "I missed you so much."

Worried he'd get the wrong idea, I twisted to face him, looped my arms around his lower back. "I mean, I missed everything, Quinn. Not just the sex—I missed everything about you. I missed laughing with you, talking with you. I missed falling asleep next to you at night and waking up with you in the morning."

"You did?" He sounded surprised. "You won't even let me touch you when you're falling asleep."

"I know, but it's more…" I thought for a second. "It's just knowing you're there. That you'll be there the next day. I like that feeling, and I never thought I would."

"Good. Because I plan on sticking around." He went back to kissing my neck. "I might never get enough of you, but I'm sure as hell going to try. Does that scare you?"

"Nope." I slid my hands down over his ass, pulling him into me. "Believe it or not, deep down I've always wanted you to try. I just wouldn't admit it. It was always you, Quinn."

He picked his head up and looked me in the eye. "It always will be."

We kissed, kicking off shoes, unzipping, unbuttoning, unhooking. We let our beautiful clothes fall to the floor where we stood, anxious to feel one another skin to skin. He pulled out my hairpins and slid his fingers into my hair. When we were naked and frantic and unsatisfied with lips and hands and tongues, craving a deeper connection, Quinn took my hand. "I want you in my bed."

He led me up the stairs and into his bedroom, a large, airy space with floor to ceiling windows and a king-sized platform bed. There was probably more furniture in the room, but I didn't notice it.

We fell onto the bed and into each other. We kissed as if it had been years, our limbs twined like ivy. I could hardly breathe, but it didn't scare me. I wanted him to smother me, wanted to suffocate on his love. "I need you," I whispered over and over again.

It was an unfamiliar kind of need, physical *and* emotional—my body demanded he fill the aching hollow inside it and my heart begged to escape my chest and be cradled by his. I looked up at him as he slid his hot, hard cock inside me, his face lit solely by the nighttime lights of the city below. "Quinn." My voice shook with the panic I felt at finally letting the feeling overtake me, at not being able to describe it.

"I know," he said, rolling over me, rocking into me as my eyes closed in ecstasy. "I feel it."

Thank God, I thought as he filled me. *Thank God I don't have to find words.* All I had were gasps and sighs, inarticulate cries of pleasure and pain, and breathless moments of agony at the peak, my hands clutching and pulling him closer, closer, closer…would it ever be enough?

And then I had tears, welling up and spilling over as our eyes locked and breath mingled and bodies contracted around one another's in a long, suspended moment of euphoric release. My fear was gone.

"I'm sorry," I wept once I could talk. "I don't know why I'm crying. I swear I'm happy."

"I know why." He kissed my forehead. "And it's OK."

"Are you going to tease me about this tomorrow?"

"No, sweet pea. I'm not."

"Thank you."

"I'm going to tease you about it for the rest of our lives."

I laughed, swatting him on the butt. "Figures."

"You OK with that?" He brushed my hair off my face.

"With what?"

"The fact that I want this for the rest of my life."

My stomach swooshed, but it was a good kind of swoosh. The kind of swoosh you feel on a rollercoaster—equal parts trepidation and excitement. "Honestly? Yes. I'm OK with that. Tonight when I made the toast, I said it was Alex and

Nolan who made me believe in love, but you know it wasn't just them."

He smiled. "I know."

"I don't know how you did it."

"I didn't, Jaime—you did. I fell in love with you, but you had to open yourself up to it. And you did."

"Eventually."

"Eventually. And I think once you felt it, you saw it in others. Not just as something beautiful but fleeting and superficial, but as something deeper."

"I did." I thought for a moment. "It's like the difference between a wedding and a marriage. A wedding is all about the show, but a marriage is about commitment you can't see. All those things you said to me at Alex's birthday finally made sense."

"Good. Does this mean you want to get married?"

My heart stopped. "You're killing me. One thing at a time, please."

"That wasn't a no. I'll take it." He kissed my lips, his tongue teasing inside them.

"I do love you, Quinn. And it *is* real, even though I've always thought you were too good to be true."

"I hope you always think that," he said, "even when I'm old and bald and fat and can't get it up anymore." He picked up his head. "Forget I said that. I'll always get it up for you."

I laughed, locking my legs around him. "I'll hold you to it, love bug."

The next morning, Quinn ran out for coffee and bagels while I lounged around his condo in one of his T-shirts. When he got back, we were going to compare calendars and check out some resorts in the Caribbean—Quinn wanted to take me on vacation, and I'd gleefully said yes.

I dug my phone out of my purse and checked messages, and then I couldn't resist checking Instagram. He'd taken a bunch of goofy pictures of me this morning, despite my protests and many a pillow thrown at his head.

Sure enough, there was one of me, but I was sleeping soundly, my dark hair a bedraggled mess on the white pillowcase, but my expression serene. He must have snuck it this morning, because the light was soft and pale.

My breath caught as I read the caption: *You know I will.*

Nothing else, no silly hashtags or jokes, just four simple words from the song we'd danced to last night, his childhood lullaby. I smiled.

Someone else might have wanted a more obvious declaration for the world to see, or maybe have wondered, you will *what?* But he knew me. And I knew I could finish it a million ways…love you, respect you, tease you, support you, laugh with you, talk to you, listen to you, stay with you. Always.

I will, too, Quinn.
I will too.

THE END

ACKNOWLEDGMENTS

To my husband and daughters, for making it possible for me to do what I love, for understanding my silences and distraction, and for reminding me how beautiful real life is.

To Jenn Watson, publicist, therapist, and so much more. I love you. Thank you for hatching me out of that egg.

To Melissa Gaston, PA/admin extraordinaire, you make my life so much easier in so many ways! You're the best!

To everyone at Social Butterfly PR, especially Hillary Suppes (congrats, new mama!) and Candi Kane (thanks for pizza, shoes, and all you do). I appreciate you!

To Rebecca Friedman, agent and friend. You are truly lovely.

To my beta readers, thank you for the feedback and encouragement.

To my proofreaders, Laura Foster Franks, Amanda Maria, Angie Owens…love your eagle eyes!

To book bloggers, who do so much for indie authors. I am so grateful—thank you, thank you, thank you, especially Give me Books for organizing Man Candy events!

To Lauren Luman (welcome to Team Harlow!) and all my Harlots for love, laughs, and lots of inspiration.

To all my readers, who know that man candy might not be nutritious, but it sure can make you feel ambitious.

MEET THE
MUSE

Meet Dima Gornovskyi, the MAN CANDY cover model and muse for Quinn Rusek! After seeing a gorgeous photograph of Dima on Facebook, I thought he'd make the perfect Quinn, and I reached out. What a delight to discover he's as sweet and smart as he is beautiful! His enthusiasm and support for MAN CANDY has been a thrill right from the start. Want to get to know him better? Read on for our Q and A!

Melanie: Hi Dima! I get so many questions about you, I thought it might be fun to put a short Q and A in the back of the book.

Dima: This is such an honor for me! Thank you :)

You were born in the Ukraine, raised in Tunisia, and now you live in LA. What feels most like home to you?

Living in L.A. is a conscious choice and so here I feel most at home more than anywhere else in the world, but I'm very grateful to have grown up in

Tunisia & Ukraine for introducing me to completely different cultures and experiences that taught me so much.

What languages do you speak?

English, Russian, Ukrainian, French, Italian and Arabic (but not all of them are good anymore) :)

Don't worry, I'm sure your Italian beats my Ukrainian by several thousand *chilometros*. You obviously work very hard to stay so fit. How do you do it?

For work, I need to be in the gym almost every day. I used to be a dancer so I love stretching and all kinds of exercises. I am also pretty strict about my diet and I have a very active life, I'm always on the go.

I love that you have dance training! OK so for a splurge, what's your favorite meal, and what would you drink with it?

I'm a huge fan of braised short ribs with a nice glass of red Zinfandel.

(Note to self, learn how to braise short ribs.) What's your favorite candy or dessert?

English Toffee ☺

What do you notice first about someone when you meet them?

How organic they are. I love when people are relaxed and natural no matter who they are or what they're doing.

What's your dream vacation?

At home with my family (I travel a lot and live far from my family so these moments are always the best).

Do you enjoy modeling? (You make it look easy, but it isn't! When I had my author photos taken, I gained new respect for people who have their picture taken constantly!)

I absolutely love it! It can be challenging at times because we are not used to seeing ourselves from different angles and perspectives, but it helps me to get out of my comfort zone.

Um, pretty sure you have no bad angles! But if you were not a model, what would you be doing?

I would be a pianist or own an advertising agency.

You play the piano too?

I used to play piano for years but when I realized that I probably wouldn't become a professional performer, I had to put it aside to develop other things. I'm absolutely in love with the piano though and I hope to come back to it when I get a little older and have more time to practice. :)

What's the craziest thing you've ever done?

I dropped my university two months after the beginning of my studies. I was supposed to become French / Chinese translator. I turned out well eventually. :)

Haha, I agree! Do you have any tattoos?

I do not. But I think tattoos are super cool. If had one, it would probably be a deer head.

You model all kinds of clothing. When you're not working, what's your favorite thing to wear?

I love the combination of navy blue and white. A good fitting pair of jeans and a T with a cool baseball hat in the daytime, and I prefer all black for a night look. Three of my favorite things in my wardrobe are: My sherpa denim jacket, Detroit baseball hat (because my name also starts with D) and my Nike sneakers.

Your Detroit baseball hat was one of the first things I noticed in your pictures! I love it—but I'm from Detroit, so I'm a little biased. ;) Quinn loves the Tigers and wears a hat like that too. This was fate! OK, so what's the best piece of advice you've ever gotten, in any language?

To never stop dreaming. I'm a dreamer and I dream big. I have all of my dreams written down in multiple places. So many of my dreams have become a reality. Another great piece of advice was to make a to-do list. I can't tell you how effective that is for me.

YOU LOVE LISTS?! Wow, we have a lot in common! Other than the fact that you are much younger and better looking and speak seven languages, I'd say we were separated at birth...yeah, maybe not. OK, I'm going to get mushy for a moment. In MAN CANDY, Quinn teases Jaime by calling her "love bug" because he

knows it bothers her. What's your favorite term of endearment to call someone you love?

Cuddle bear, but if I wanted to bother someone in a flirtatious way, I would call them a weirdo.

Hahaha, cuddle bear! That's one I didn't think of for Quinn and Jaime! Now the lightning round...

Favorite color?

Navy blue

Favorite song?

Madonna - Secret

Favorite movie?

Blue Jasmine by Woody Allen

You really do love blue! It's my favorite color, too. :) Dima, thank you so much for doing this--I truly appreciate it!

Of course, this is so much fun for me!!

Thanks for reading!

ABOUT THE AUTHOR

Melanie Harlow likes her heels high, her hair pink, and her history with the naughty bits left in. In addition to MAN CANDY, she's the author of the HAPPY CRAZY LOVE series (contemporary romance), the FRENCHED series (contemporary romance) and the SPEAK EASY duet (historical romance). She writes from her home outside of Detroit, where she lives with her husband, two daughters, and one insane rabbit.

Connect with Melanie online:

Website: www.melanieharlow.com

Facebook: www.facebook.com/AuthorMelanieHarlow

Email: melanieharlowwrites@gmail.com

OTHER BOOKS BY
MELANIE HARLOW

The Frenched Series
Frenched
Yanked (a *Frenched* novella)
Forked
Floored

The Happy Crazy Love Series
Some Sort of Happy
Some Sort of Crazy
Some Sort of Love

The Speak Easy Duet
Speak Easy
Speak Low

The Tango Lesson (a standalone novella)

Printed in Great Britain
by Amazon